TANGLED UP IN HATE

CHARLOTTE BYRD

Epic love requires an epic sacrifice...

A long time ago, I borrowed money from a very powerful family. I paid my debt, but they have come for more.

They want everything that I have built and they will hurt her if I refuse.

Harley doesn't understand why I have to break her heart. She hates me, but at least she's okay...for now.

But what happens when sending her away isn't enough?

What happens when I lose everything?

"Fast-paced, dark, addictive, and compelling" - Amazon Reviewer ★★★★★

"Hot, steamy, and a great storyline." - Christine Reese ★★★★★

"My oh my....Charlotte has made me a fan for life." - JJ, Amazon Reviewer ★★★★★

"The tension and chemistry is at five alarm level." - Sharon, Amazon reviewer ★★★★★

"Hot, sexy, intriguing journey of Elli and Mr. Aiden Black. - Robin Langelier ★★★★★

"Wow. Just wow. Charlotte Byrd leaves me speechless and humble... It definitely kept me on the edge of my seat. Once you pick it up, you won't put it down." - Amazon Review
★★★★★

"Sexy, steamy and captivating!" - Charmaine, Amazon Reviewer ★★★★★

" Intrigue, lust, and great characters...what more

could you ask for?!" - Dragonfly Lady
★★★★★

"An awesome book. Extremely entertaining, captivating and interesting sexy read. I could not put it down." - Kim F, Amazon Reviewer
★★★★★

"Just the absolute best story. Everything I like to read about and more. Such a great story I will read again and again. A keeper!!" - Wendy Ballard ★★★★★

"It had the perfect amount of twists and turns. I instantaneously bonded with the heroine and of course Mr. Black. YUM. It's sexy, it's sassy, it's steamy. It's everything." - Khardine Gray, Bestselling Romance Author ★★★★★

DON'T MISS OUT!

Want to be the first to know about my upcoming sales, new releases and exclusive giveaways?

Sign up for my Newsletter and join my Reader Club!

Bonus Points: Follow me on BookBub!

ALSO BY CHARLOTTE BYRD

All books are available at ALL major retailers!
If you can't find it, please email me at
charlotte@charlotte-byrd.com

Black Series
Black Edge
Black Rules
Black Bounds
Black Contract
Black Limit

House of York Trilogy
House of York
Crown of York
Throne of York

Standalone Novels

Debt

Offer

Unknown

Dressing Mr. Dalton

1

JACKSON

BEFORE...

"Tell me, what is it you plan to do with your one wild and precious life?"

I read the words over and over again silently.

And when that's not enough, I repeat them out loud.

Our life is a gift.

A precious and wild gift from the universe. It doesn't matter if you believe in reincarnation or an all-knowing God, we all come from dust and we will return to dust.

And then there's our time here.

Here on Earth.

Of course.

What is it that you plan to do with your one *wild* and *precious* life, Jackson? I ask myself.

I look at myself in the mirror.

The man looking back at me is attractive, and distinguished, and rich.

The world is mine, so to speak, I can do anything I want. Or so it seems on the outside. On the inside, however, my life isn't so easy.

There are complications.

My business.

My obligations to everyone who works there.

So, I can't just take off. I can't just put it to one side and do something else.

But there's an even bigger problem than that.

What is it that I would do if I could do anything?

There was a time when building my company up from nothing meant the world to me.

Every quarter we made more and more revenue and we brought in more and more advertisers.

My life became fueled by the numbers on the ledger.

My life revolved around our profit-loss statements. It was all I thought about all day and all night.

I certainly didn't want to think about anything else.

If I did, then I'd have to think about living my life entirely cut off from everything that is human.

Then I'd have to think about what it would be like to have real friends again.

And what it would be like to fall in love again, or at least open myself up to the possibility of opening myself up to another person.

I thought that I had it all figured out.

I thought that if I could barricade myself in my mansion then nothing could hurt me.

And I was right, for a bit.

But as time passed and months became years, something else dawned on me.

It wasn't so much that I was keeping the rest of the world out, but keeping myself in.

My home has become a prison of my own making and after a while, I wasn't strong enough to escape that world.

Until her.

Harley Burke.

Chestnut hair.

Inquisitive eyes.

Plump lips and a square jaw.

Sometimes she smirks when she laughs and sometimes, she even snorts.

But most of the time, her laughter sounds like angels singing.

Harley Burke burst into my life, freeing me from a cage of my own design.

She brought me out into the world and she showed me that it's not as scary as I thought that it would be.

She showed me that life is not only precious and wild but also kind.

She showed me what it feels to get that shock of electricity coursing through your body when you think about someone coming over soon.

She challenged me.

But mostly, she taught me how to believe in not only love, but also life.

I had lost faith in life for a while there, and she showed me that reality has a lot to do with how you look at it.

Two people can experience the same exact terrible thing, but what changes everything is their perception of that thing.

And so, that's why I'm here now.

Harley showed me that life is wild and precious and what I want to do now with mine is to go out there and buy her a ring.

I don't know where she is. I don't know if she's even alive, but I am buying a ring because I believe.

She will come back to me.

And when she does, I will use this ring to propose to her.

Why now?

There comes a point when you realize that all you want is to spend the rest of your life with one person.

And when that point comes, you also realize that you want the rest of your life to start as soon as possible.

This phrase comes from *When Harry Met Sally*, and I butchered it, of course.

But the reason I mention it here is that I never really understood what it meant until the moment when the realization dawned on me.

Instead of heading to Tiffany's or Harry Winston or another well-known brand, I go to the small office of a jeweler I found on Etsy.

She's a woman in her late thirties and she

recognizes me immediately when I walk in but does not mention it.

Instead, she shows me the kind of floating diamond rings that I mentioned I would like for Harley and explains the different things about various setting options.

I don't know much about diamonds and I appreciate the introductory lesson. After I decide on a three-carat diamond, emerald cut, with side diamonds, set in platinum, she gives me an estimated price of fifteen grand.

It's about half of the price I've seen for a similar ring online and about a fourth even, not more, of the cost of the same ring from a jeweler with an international brand.

I'm not here because I'm trying to save money.

I'm here because I know that this is where Harley would like me to get her ring - from a small jeweler with amazing online reviews who runs her own business.

I pay the deposit and thank her for her time.

"Thank you so much, Mr. Ludlow. I know that you won't be disappointed," she says.

"I know. Thank *you*."

Stepping back out into the cold, I finally

know the answer to that question that Mary Oliver asked in her poem.

What is it you plan to do with your one wild and precious life?

To find Harley, and to do everything in my power to make her happy.

2

HARLEY

THE SMELL OF PAPER…

Used bookstores make my heart ache, in a good way.

They are stuffy and smelly and claustrophobic, but that's also what's magical about them.

They aren't like new bookstores where everything is organized just perfectly and you can find any book that you are looking for.

Those are good, too, especially if you also want a cup of coffee and a scone, and the peace of mind to sit and read for hours.

But it's the used bookstores that really captivate me. I think it's because they are full of the unknown.

You can go in there with an idea of a book

you're looking for, and you may find it, especially if it's a classic or popular.

But what's even better than that is to go in there with a completely open mind. Without even a notion of what you may want.

That's when the real adventure begins.

I wander around the aisles, running my fingertips over the old spines.

Some are old, others are ancient.

And others are almost new.

I'm not looking for anything in particular, but I am looking for something that will draw me in.

I know you're not supposed to judge a book by its cover, but what else do you have to go by?

Especially if you have never heard of the author or the title before?

Something makes me stop by the poetry section.

I've never read many poems before. I pull out one of the newer books from the shelf and stare at the cover.

It doesn't really speak to me.

It's devoid of all color, except black and white, and has a middle-aged woman glancing strangely back at me.

She's not particularly attractive, but she's also

not particularly unattractive. Her boyish haircut isn't doing her any favors.

I'm about to put it back, but something stops me.

Instead, I open it. Not to the beginning, but to a random page.

Listen—are you breathing just a little, and calling it a life?

The words catch me by surprise. More than that really.

They stop me in my tracks completely.

I read the words over and over again until they are ingrained onto my soul.

How could this poet grab ahold of me with just a question and change the way I see everything about myself?

My answer?

Yes, I am breathing just a little and calling it a life. But not starting from this moment.

Now, every time I feel myself falling into the abyss of everyday life, it's going to change. I'm more than just a person who goes to work, pays the bills, and thinks about things that I should be doing that I'm not.

The thing is that I know exactly what I should be doing.

I should be writing.

That's what I really want to do with my life.

But mundane things tend to get in the way of that.

There are always emails to answer. More jobs to take to pay the bills. And after all of that is done, I'm just tired.

Too tired to do the one thing that I really want to spend my time doing. Not after today, I promise myself. Things are going to change.

I will no longer breathe just a little and call it a life.

My life will be full of passion and adventure.

I take the book to the checkout counter. The woman behind the register smiles at me.

"Mary Oliver, one of my favorite poets," she says, scanning my book.

"I've never read her before," I admit as I hand her a five-dollar bill.

"She's going to change your life."

She already has.

I BOUGHT Mary Oliver's book of poetry a year before I met Jackson.

I came home that night and devoured the book and promised myself that in the morning, I'm going to start writing.

But I didn't. I set the alarm for six so I could get some writing in before I had to officially begin work, but it was too early and I never got up. I was going to write after work, but again I was too tired.

After making dinner, all I wanted to do was pass out in front of the television. Within a week, I put Mary Oliver's book away.

It was just a painful reminder of everything that I should be doing, and that I was too distracted to do.

I hated how guilty it made me feel. The words that once spoke to my very core, now made me rot from the inside out.

That is until I started writing fiction again. This time, it wasn't the book that inspired me.

It was Jackson.

He encouraged me.

He supported me.

And he gave me the time to do it. When I no longer had to work to make money, suddenly, I couldn't stop writing.

All I wanted to do all day was work on my novel.

And when it was done, I wanted to start the continuation of the story.

Jackson leans over my shoulder and looks at the screen.

"Wow." He gives me a peck on the top of my head.

My face freezes in a smile.

"How many units is that?" he asks.

I click on the bar graph. "Thirty-seven," I whisper, careful not to break the spell.

"You sold thirty-seven books today?"

"Uh-huh."

"Well, come here." He pulls me up to my feet and kisses me passionately on the mouth. I kiss him right back.

"I couldn't do this without you," I mumble.

"Of course, you could. It was you who did it."

"But you supported me. You believed in me."

"That's what you do when you love someone."

I wrap my arms around his neck, draping myself over him. He tries to lead me to the bed, but I pull away.

"No…" I laugh.

"What? Why?"

"Because I have work to do. I need to finish this chapter."

"I have created a monster," Jackson says, pulling me in for one more kiss.

3

HARLEY

WHEN I CAN'T PULL AWAY...

I want to pull away again.

I have work to do.

But with Jackson's arms around me, I lose myself.

It's as if another part of me takes over. I am no longer ruled by my mind, but by my body.

My arms wrap around his neck on their own as my legs walk backward toward the bed.

I pull him on top of me and my body quivers under his.

His muscles are powerful and strong and I bury my fingernails into his back. Our lips devour each other's but then he pulls away from me for a second.

"I thought you had to work," he mocks.

"I thought I did, too," I mumble and pull him closer to me.

I open my mouth and welcome his tongue inside.

Tugging at his shirt, I pull it over his head.

With our faces briefly separated, I bite my lower lip as I run my fingertips over his washboard abs.

They flex and relax with each breath.

He pulls my chin up to his face and says, "My eyes are up here."

I laugh. "You're just so...delicious."

"Delicious, huh? I would have to say the same thing about you as well."

He pins me down to the bed with my hands behind my head.

I smile.

He presses his lips to mine and slowly makes his way down my neck and to the top of my breasts.

I am still wearing a long sleeve V-neck, but not for long.

When he pulls it off, I reach down and unbuckle his belt.

"What's the hurry?" he whispers in my ear.

"I want you right now," I say and pull off my own leggings along with my underwear.

I kiss him again.

Our kisses are sloppy and messy and neither of us really care.

"How do you want to do it?" he mumbles into my ear.

I flip over on my stomach and put my butt up in the air.

Jackson laughs, grabbing me by my hips and pushing me back down to the bed.

I bury my face in the pillow, only turning my neck slightly to get some air.

The silk sheets keep slipping through my fingers every time I try to grab hold of them.

As he slides into me, I revel in his body cradling mine.

It's as if he is draped completely around me, protecting us in an impenetrable cocoon.

With each movement, a warm soothing sensation starts to build within my body. I feel myself getting close, shut my eyes, and try to relax and lose myself in the moment.

But then he grabs onto my hair and pulls me back off the bed.

It's just an inch or so and it's not painful.

The sensation makes my whole body ache for his and the moment that I thought I could prolong takes me over completely.

I yell his name into my pillow, wrapping my fingers around the corners of it. Jackson continues to move on top of me.

The tempo increases along with his breathing until he can't hold on anymore than I could.

I close my eyes as I listen to him whisper my name and collapse on top of me, completely spent.

Suddenly, a pang of fear rushes through me.

"Oh my God," I whisper, pushing him off me. "We didn't use anything."

He smiles and starts to laugh.

My brows furrow in anger.

How could he do this?

He knows that I'm not on the pill.

How could he be so irresponsible?

Though I'm directing my frustration outward, it really belongs with me. It is me who I am angry with.

You're not a fucking teenager, Harley.

You need to think.

But Jackson doesn't seem to share my concern.

Instead, he paints a stupid, plastic smile on his face and laughs.

"What am I going to do?" I shove him, wrapping the sheet around my body. "Why are you laughing?"

He points down.

"What?"

"Look." He continues to point down. Finally, I look where he's signaling and crack up as well.

"You should've seen your face," he says, giving me a kiss.

"You shouldn't play games like that."

"I wasn't playing a game."

I kiss him back.

"How did you even get it on so quickly? I didn't see you doing it at all," I say.

"What can I say? I've got skills."

HARLEY

WHEN WE DISAGREE...

The bodyguards are following us around everywhere.

I think it's a bit of overkill, but Jackson has decided that it's absolutely necessary. In the house, they pretty much leave me alone.

Yet, when I go outside, they don't leave my side.

Why does it bother me so much?

Why can't I just ignore it, like Jackson has suggested on a number of occasions? Believe me, I tried.

But I can't.

Their mere presence, watching me, following me everywhere I go feels like I have a stalker again.

"Parker Huntington is a very dangerous person," Jackson says when I bring up going to the bookstore on my own.

We are still lying in bed, in the afterglow of our afternoon's delight.

"Are you seriously telling me this?" I ask, sitting up, and pulling the sheet over my breasts. "You don't think I know that?"

"He's still out there. The police don't know where he is. The FBI is looking for him. And he's looking for you."

"You don't know that."

"Yes, I do."

"He's probably thousands of miles away from here by now. He's not an idiot," I insist. "He doesn't want to go to prison."

Jackson shakes his head with a disappointed look on his face.

I get out of bed, frustrated.

This is not how our amazing afternoon today should've ended, with this bitter taste in both of our mouths.

After all of this time together, and through everything that we have been through, this is really the only point of contention that we have.

I don't want anyone following me and he does. He doesn't trust the world and thinks that these people will protect me.

It's not that I trust the world much, or that I don't think that the bodyguards aren't good at their job.

It's more that I want my freedom.

After being held captive in that God-forsaken cabin, I want to go where I please and do what I want. I don't want to report to anyone. I don't want to account for myself in any way.

After I put on my clothes, I pick up the laptop and head into my favorite room. It's the downstairs study, with beautiful blush pink walls and bookcases that line the bottom half of the room.

It has large windows and a soft gray fabric couch.

Sitting down, I prop my feet up on the matching ottoman and glance out of the window.

A little blackbird hops on the windowsill, inquisitively peering inside.

I try to put our argument out of my mind and distract myself with something else.

There's a string of unopened emails, most of which I delete without even opening.

I should really unsubscribe myself from these lists instead of deleting them every day, but today will not be the day for that project.

I LOVE YOUR BOOK!

I STARE at the subject line in disbelief.

Is this really from a reader?

My hands get sweaty and my heartbeat speeds up a bit.

I try to click on the headline slowly, but it's either a click or not.

I take a deep breath before reading the body of the email.

Wow! I love this story so much. I was supposed to clean and meal-prep today, but instead I stayed curled up on the couch reading your book. I can't wait to get back to it tonight after I put the kids to bed. Thank you so much for writing it! When is the next one coming out?

.   .   .

MY BODY TREMBLES as I read the words over and over.

She loved my book? Really?

Enough to actually reach out to me and tell me? I have been moved by books before, of course.

But it never really occurred to me to reach out to the writer and tell her about it. And when Jackson insisted that I make the newsletter sign up and post my author email in the back of my books and on my author profile online, it never once occurred to me that anyone would ever reach out.

I write her back almost immediately.

THANK YOU SO MUCH! Your email is everything!! I am so glad you enjoyed my book. I am currently working on the second book and it should be out in a week or two.

AND AS SOON AS I press send, I turn back to my book and start writing.

The words flow fast and steady.

It takes me a good ten minutes to focus my mind at first, but then my body seems to take over.

It's as if my fingers type on their own, and all my mind has to do is follow along.

Everybody knows about writer's block and I am not immune to it.

At least, in my past. I would sit in front of the blank page for hours, spending most of that time distracting myself with my phone and the internet.

But no more.

When I started writing this series, I realized that the most important key to writing is to place your butt in a chair and force yourself to do it.

Easier said than done, huh?

Well, there are a few more tricks to it.

They may not work for everyone, but they have worked for me.

I never start writing without having a really good idea of what I'm going to cover in this chapter.

In fact, I always write down a few sentences of what's going to happen right below where the chapter begins.

Another thing I do is time myself.

It's always hardest to write the first one thousand words early in the morning. So, I set the timer and lie to myself.

Just write for twenty minutes.

That's it. Just do that and that will be it.

I read over the paragraph of what I'm going to write about and then start the clock.

Well, with the timer running, my competitive nature kicks in.

My mind starts to formulate thoughts and my fingers begin to type.

Quickly, the page gets filled up with words.

Usually, by the time the timer goes off, I am well into my creative flow zone and I want nothing more than to keep going.

So, I do.

But if, after twenty minutes, I still feel like I'm dragging my feet, then I set the timer again.

And again.

That's the thing about writing.

It's an art form, of course. But it's also a sport.

It requires constant exercise and engagement.

All I ever wanted to do was write, so that's exactly what I'm doing.

And now that I have this opportunity, now that people are actually buying my books and writing me emails about how much they love them, I want to do it even more. It's all I really want to do.

5

HARLEY

WHEN HE SURPRISED ME...

After finishing two thousand words, I take a little break.

I'm thirsty and a bit hungry but I avoid the kitchen.

That's where the bodyguards tend to congregate and I hate seeing them here. Though the house is big enough to wander through it without really noticing them, I know that they're here.

And that's what irks me.

At the top of the stairs, I immediately turn to the east wing of the house because that's where our bedroom is.

But something stops me.

I've actually never seen the other side of this floor.

There is a reason for that. I remember it clearly.

It was my first day here and Jackson had specifically forbid me to go to the upper west wing of the house.

And I haven't.

Not yet.

Now, it's okay, right?

I mean, I'm not an employee anymore.

I'm a girlfriend.

I practically live here now.

So, it often feels like I am a lot more than that. I walk to the end of the hall and try one of the rooms.

When I twist the handle, the door opens and I walk into an office. Or maybe it's a library.

There are shelves going up to the ceiling, all around the large desk in the middle of the room. The desk is lined with photographs.

Lila.

So, this is her. I pick up a silver frame with a little girl in pigtails on a tricycle. She has Jackson's smile.

In another picture, she's swinging on a rope swing.

In another, she is walking barefoot on the beach, laughing.

I look at each one and run my fingers over her face.

In all of this time that we have been together, through everything that we have endured, he has only mentioned her name a handful of times.

I poured my heart out to him in Montana, telling him of my own loss.

But he has hidden his pain from me.

It's more than that actually. He has hidden his pain away from himself.

I only know bits and pieces of what happened.

But being in this room, it's suddenly clear.

There's the fireplace.

I touch the ornate woodwork on the mantel.

It's beautiful, but it's not original.

It has been replaced since the fire.

I try to piece together the sequence of events from what Jackson told me. But it all comes in pieces.

One moment, Lila was playing here and the next she was ablaze.

Did she get too close to the fire?

Did one of the sparks fly too far away from the wood?

Questions twirl around in my head, but then another one dawns on me.

Does it really matter?

She's gone and so is the man who was her father. Jackson is still himself in body, and most of his soul, but there's a hole there.

When I first met him, I thought that empty space within him could mend somehow. I thought that by bringing him out into the world, he would get all better. And a big part of him did.

But there is still this speck, this little piece that's not quite the same.

I know because there's a part of me that's not quite the same.

"What are you doing here?"

His thunderous voice startles me and I drop the copper picture frame with Lila running through a field in a big white dress.

The glass shatters as it hits the floor and shards go everywhere.

"I'm so sorry," I mumble, getting down on my knees to try to salvage the picture.

"What the fuck are you doing here?" Jackson demands.

He has never cursed at me before. The word sends shivers down my spine.

"I'm sorry, okay? I've never been here before...I was just looking around."

He grabs me by my shoulders, pulling me up to my feet.

"You're not allowed here. Don't you remember that?"

"Yes, but I thought that..." My words trail off.

"I don't want you here. This is my private space."

He ushers me to the door, but I resist. I know that he's angry, but that his rage is fueled by sorrow.

"This is where it happened, isn't it?" I whisper.

"I don't want to talk about it. You have to leave."

"Let me just clean the glass. It's the least I can do," I plead.

Our eyes meet and suddenly it occurs to me that this is a much bigger deal than it seemed. There's a darkness there. His gaze isn't like it was before. Something is different.

I apologize again and again.

I reach for his hand, but he pushes me away.

When he finally gets me out of that room, he closes the door behind us and locks it.

I wait for whatever is going to happen next.

He just needs some time.

I'll give him some space and everything will be back to normal.

I just know it.

He's angry, but it's nothing that can't be fixed.

"I'm sorry," I whisper again and put my arms around him.

He takes a deep breath and exhales slowly.

Then he pulls away from me and focuses his gaze on mine.

"This isn't going to work, Harley." His words are slow.

Deliberate.

Final.

"I need you to take your things and move out."

6

HARLEY

WHEN NOTHING MAKES SENSE...

My ears start to buzz as a thick haze forms in front of my eyes.

Suddenly, I'm in a fog.

Nothing makes sense.

What is he talking about?

I stare at him in disbelief.

"Don't even joke about that, Jackson," I say, taking a step toward him.

I put my hand on his chest.

He lets me linger there for a moment before pushing me away.

"Do you hear me?" I ask. "I don't want to be one of those couples who threaten to break up over every little thing. We can't be those people."

He doesn't say anything for a moment.

I wait for him to respond.

Then I wait some more.

There's something scary in his silence.

I haven't seen this before.

The expression on his face changes and a new seriousness settles in between his eyebrows.

Everything about him is tense.

Clenched up.

Hidden away from me.

"If you don't want me here, I won't come in here again," I say quietly and walk toward the door.

This is going to be fine.

He didn't mean that.

But he's also not in a position to talk.

Something is looming over him.

It's a dark cloud that fills the whole room, sucking it of oxygen.

"I meant what I said, Harley," Jackson says quietly.

Again, his words are short and deliberate.

Focused.

It's as if he means every one.

But I know that he can't.

No, he doesn't want to break up with me.

He just made love to me.

He just told me how much I mean to him.

Where is this coming from? What happened?

"Why? What are you talking about?" I ask. My voice comes out cracked and high-pitched. I cough to make the lump in the back of my throat go away, but it doesn't.

"Why are you doing this?" I plead.

But he turns away from me.

I walk over to him and forcibly turn him to face me.

He can't get away with this.

He can't just break my heart and break everything that is real and true between us and walk away without an explanation.

His eyes have no life in them.

I press him closer to me and I force my lips onto his.

But he pushes me away.

I stumble.

He catches me, picks me up, and plants me on my feet as if I were a child.

"What are you doing?" I whisper, tears flowing down my face. "What is going on? Whatever it is we can fix it."

"I... just...don't want to be with you anymore," he says quietly. He pauses slightly in between the words as if saying them requires a feat of enormous strength.

"Why? You have to tell me why!"

"No, I don't."

I clench my fists and throw them at his chest. He lets me pound him for a moment then grabs me by my wrists and holds them out.

"Calm down."

But I can't.

My whole body is shaking, and my legs seem to give out under me.

When he lets me go, I collapse onto the floor.

The world starts to spin around me.

I'm on one of those amusement rides where you go as fast as you can around a fixed point and your only goal once you get on is to just hold on as tight as possible to get through it in one piece.

So, that's what I do. I hold on and wait for the centripetal force to take me away from here.

Somewhere in the distance I hear him again.

He is far away and getting even further with each word.

"Please take all of your stuff and leave. Martin will see you out and help you get home. I have loaded this card with enough money to last you a long time. Martin's fee is already paid and he will protect you when you need to go somewhere."

The door slams shut behind me, leaving me alone in this forbidden place.

I hang my head and let the tears run down my cheeks with abandon.

I don't push them away, I just watch them come.

Whatever pain I felt before when I left him is nothing compared to this.

This one feels like a butcher knife going into my body over and over again. Just as I think I can take another breath another pang of pain rips me apart.

The tears don't stop, but after a while I manage to stagger up to my feet.

I glance at the desk.

Is this why he did it?

Because I went into this wing?

Because I intruded into his past?

Because I dared to look at some pictures of Lila?

He wouldn't let me clean up the broken glass on the floor.

But he was foolish enough to leave me here.

I grab the silver picture frame and launch it toward the wall.

It shatters against the bookshelf, sending little pieces of glass in all directions.

I close my eyes after a few pieces hit my face.

I like the feeling of this destruction.

If I can't mend our love, I will destroy it.

I grab another picture frame and throw it at the rest.

I want to make him feel as badly as he made me feel.

But I know that it won't.

Everything here can be replaced.

And I can't replace us.

"What are you doing?" Martin runs in, grabbing the largest frame from my hand and throwing it to the floor.

"This doesn't concern you."

"You cannot do this, Harley," he says, wrapping his arms around me and pulling me away from the desk. "You need to calm down."

"Fuck you!"

He forces me out to the hallway once and for all, letting me go to lock the door behind us. I run toward the staircase.

I collide into the banister, and the top part of me leans slightly over the edge. I look down.

What would it take to just jump?

Nothing.

Nothing at all.

7

HARLEY

WHEN I CONSIDER THE IMPOSSIBLE...

"What are you doing?" Martin pulls me away.

I start to laugh.

He takes a step away from me in confusion.

"What did you think? I was going to jump? Because of that asshole? He wishes," I say confidently.

I don't know if Martin believes me, but I'm so certain that I practically believe it myself.

But the truth is that I almost did.

Just on impulse.

Just because it was the only thing that might have made me feel better. Maybe it wouldn't make me feel better, but it would definitely make me feel nothing.

And that would've been an improvement.

"You're bleeding," Martin points out.

I follow his gaze to my arm.

The cuts don't look like they're deep, but the blood spilling out of them is crimson.

After examining the wounds and convincing himself that there are no shards of glass in them, Martin takes off his shirt and wraps it around my arm.

I watch him do this in third person. I'm not really here.

This isn't really my body.

None of this is really happening. It's just a bad dream from which I'm going to wake up any minute now.

I wait.

I wait.

I wait some more, but nothing happens.

Martin leads me to our bedroom and shows me a paper box where I should put all of my stuff.

I don't have much.

A laptop.

A notebook.

Some clothes, but they are half unpacked in the carry on suitcase in the closet.

I pack that up as well and Martin carries it all for me.

"Don't forget this," he says, handing me the card that Jackson left in the office.

Somehow he had managed to take it while ushering me out of the door.

"What is that?" I ask, even though I know exactly what it is.

"Mr. Ludlow wanted you to have it."

"Mr. Ludlow is an asshole."

"That may be so, but you don't want to leave this here."

I stare at him and roll my eyes.

"He had me put a lot of money on it. Here's the receipt."

He pulls out a crumpled piece of paper from his pocket. I glance at the figure at the bottom.

"He had you put a hundred grand on it?"

Martin nods.

"Why?"

"He said to just let him know if you need more and he'll add to it."

"Why?"

"Because he wanted you to have the money. To live. To pay for stuff."

I shake my head. "No, no, no. That's not what he wanted."

Martin nods.

"He didn't want to feel bad for dumping me. So, he thought that he could just pay me off. As if I were a hooker."

Martin shakes his head.

"You don't believe me?"

"Please take the money, Harley. It's a lot of money. You deserve it."

The word 'deserve' sticks with me. What is he talking about? What does he know?

"Why?" I ask.

But then he clams up and turns away. "Mr. Ludlow knows your financial situation and he wants you to be...comfortable."

"You and I both know that he's just trying to wash away his sins. He thinks that if he pays me then it's okay that he broke up with me for no reason. He thinks this will make everything better. And you know what annoys me the most? That I always thought that he wasn't like the rest of those wealthy, rich as fuck assholes. I always thought that he was different. That he didn't think that his money bought everything in the world. Well, I was wrong. I was wrong about many things."

THE REST of the day is a blur.

Martin takes me back to my old apartment with Julie.

He brings my stuff in with me and I go straight to my bed and curl up under the covers.

I want to take a shower to wash all of this ugliness from me, but I don't have the strength.

I put on my headphones, put on some instrumental music, and cover my eyes with my eye mask.

I drift off to sleep and when I wake up sometime later, I hear Julie and Martin talking in hushed tones in the kitchen.

The room is dark and I turn the music up louder and close my eyes again.

Being awake is a reminder of everything that I have lost.

I want to go to sleep, but salty tears start to run down my cheeks instead.

I bury my face in the pillow to muffle my sobs.

"I should go comfort her." I hear Julie say somewhere in the distance.

"Just give her some space," someone else says. Who? Oh, yes, Martin. That phantom of a man who brought me here.

"No, I should," she whispers.

Don't, I pray.

Leave me alone.

I don't want anyone here.

I just need to lose myself in my own sorrow.

I cover my head with the blanket and turn more into the wall.

The fetal position is supposed to be comforting, but it's not. It rouses me out of my sleep and makes my mind run again.

Memories of him come flooding back.

His hand on mine.

Palm to palm.

Our fingers intertwining.

His kisses as soft as a butterfly's.

His full lips.

His sparkling eyes.

The soft way he said my name when he wanted to bring me closer to him. The loud way he screamed my name when he was inside of me.

It wasn't that long ago that I thought that we would be together forever. He's standing in front of me at my parents' wedding, mouthing 'I love you' over and over.

I was so certain then.

He walked around as if he had a secret to hide, a good one.

The one he couldn't wait to share with me.

I knew deep down that he was going to ask me to marry him. I couldn't wait to say yes.

But now I know what the secret was, he was planning on breaking everything off.

The past rushes into the present, painting everything black.

8

JACKSON

WHEN I DO THE IMPOSSIBLE...

I hear her typing.

There's a happy twang to it.

The words seem to be spilling out of her as she loses herself in that imaginary world that gives so much meaning to her life.

As I listen to her write, I hope that she doesn't forget how this makes her feel when I hurt her.

The thought of doing it makes my body shudder.

Every cell in me fights against it.

I know it's wrong.

It's the last thing I want to do.

But it's also the only thing I can do to protect her.

That's why I'm doing this. It's the only reason.

She's going to hate me.

She's going to want an explanation, but if I don't extricate myself from the situation fast enough, if I don't just pull off the bandage all at once, the pain will be too unbearable.

But worse than that.

If I start to explain then I might tell her the truth.

This is one thing she must not know.

This is the one thing that I have to keep to myself.

Again, it's to protect her.

This is the only way.

I look for her in her favorite working place, the pink room, but she's not there. I check everywhere downstairs and then head back to our bedroom. Please don't be there, I say to myself over and over again.

I can't do this there. That place is our home. I can still smell her hair on the pillow cases. No, that place has too many memories.

I look around and again she is nowhere to be found.

Where are you? I wonder. My feet take me to

the west wing. She won't be here. I told her this place was off limits.

Through the crack in the door, I see her.

She's holding Lila's picture in her hand.

My heart drops. My breathing slows down. I freeze.

I told her bits and pieces of what happened.

But I never told her the whole story.

She knows about the fireplace and she knows about the fire.

What more is there to tell?

Suddenly, everything about this room seems ridiculous.

There was a time when I couldn't even go in here, but now? Now, I'm going to do the impossible here.

From now on, this will not just be the room where I lost my baby girl. This will also be the room where I lost my soul mate.

Don't do it, my body screams. I clench my fists. Tears start to well up in my eyes, but I push them away with force.

I feel myself become completely rigid.

I straighten my spine and square my shoulders.

My eyes deaden.

My breathing slows down.

She apologizes for being in the room. She tries to make amends. But none of that can stop the moving train. I have to do what I have to do. I have to say the words. I open my mouth once, but they don't come. Harley Burke is the love of my life. I cannot imagine my life without her. I cannot do this. But if I want her to live then I have to. Being apart is a sacrifice I have to make. It's the only thing that is going save her. Protect her. Allow her to live the rest of her life free of danger.

They cannot know that she means anything to me. It's the only way out. It's the only way she'll be safe.

I take a deep breath. I gather my courage. You have to do this, Jackson, I say to myself. You have to do this now.

"This isn't going to work, Harley," I say. "I need you to take your things and move out."

THERE ARE moments in life which separate a before and an after.

There was a time before Lila was born when

I was young and free and not a parent. And then after she came into this world and made me a dad.

After her death, everything that happened became a before. But then I met Harley and I thought that this would be the only after I would ever have again. Our love was going to last happily ever after.

But reality struck again.

As she sobs and pounds on me, demanding an explanation, I tense myself up, refusing to let any of her pain in. If I let go just a little, then I won't be able to go through with this. Then I'll cave and tell her the truth and she won't go.

I have already experienced what it would be like to not have her in the world and I can't go through that again. I couldn't live with myself if I knew that she was dead because of me.

She continues to pound against me. She continues to fight. And then her legs start to collapse under her. She can't stand anymore and no matter how hard I try to prop her up again, it doesn't work.

It's time to go. I turn away from her and leave. When the door closes behind me, I stand here listening to her sobs, fighting every intention in my body to go back there and take her into my arms.

But I have seen what they are capable of. I have seen the dead bodies that they left in their wake and Harley cannot be one of those people with a bullet through her head. Not if there's something I can do about it.

Through the door, I hear her break Lila's picture frames. The undeniable sound of shattering glass fills the room. Martin reaches for the door, but I stop him.

"Not yet."

We stand listening to her devastation.

"Okay, now," I say and open the door for him then walk away.

9

JACKSON

AFTERMATH...

I get sick to my stomach as soon as it's done.
I run to the bathroom and bury my face in the toilet. When I come up for air, I take a breath and get sick again.

And again.

I throw up until my insides burn. I throw up until I can't throw up anymore. But still it's not enough.

Still, I can't seem to get this sickness out of me. This darkness that settled somewhere deep within me.

I know that I will not be free of it until Harley is back in my life, and that means I'll have it with me forever.

I stagger to the bed.

Her scent is everywhere.

The memory of her walks through this house as a ghost. Everywhere I look, there she is, wondering why I broke her heart.

I close my eyes to shut out the questions, but it's not enough. I bury my head in the pillows and throw the cover over my head.

Finally, the world is as dark as I feel.

I WAKE up a few hours later with my head pounding and my body shivering. I am drenched in sweat.

Climbing out of bed, I force myself to change my clothes to warm up. In the closet, I find a pair of sweatpants and am careful not to look where her suitcase once stood.

I need to rid this place of her memory, but if I do that, what will I have left?

I finally start to warm up when I put on a long sleeve shirt, a hoodie, and a pair of thick socks.

When I come downstairs, twilight has started to fall. Evening is about to come, my first night without Harley.

I have spent other nights without her, of course, but this one will be different. This one will have a finality to it that I'm not sure I will be able to handle.

I find Aurora in the kitchen.

Her head is buried in the refrigerator. She knows nothing about this, but if I tell her then she'll know why I had to do this.

I debate whether I should.

Maybe I need to keep this to myself entirely. Maybe she needs protection, too. I don't know. She moved out a week ago. She has a new boyfriend.

"I have to tell you something," I start. I'm justifying my reasons for telling her, mainly because I need to tell someone who would understand.

"I broke up with Harley," I say.

"Oh...okay." She nods. She has always been good about not pushing me for answers I'm not ready to give. Instead, she just waits. Here's my chance to protect her. Just lie to her. Tell her it's nothing personal, it just wasn't working out. Things happen. If anyone were to understand that, it would be Aurora.

"The Lindells threatened me."

Her face loses all color. "What do you mean?"

"They think they deserve fifty percent of my company. Because of something they did all those years ago."

"Didn't you pay them back?"

I nod.

"Plus another hundred grand as a thank you. But they don't think it's enough."

"This isn't fair." Aurora shakes her head. That was my initial reaction as well.

"Of course not. They're the Lindells and they take what they want."

"So...what are you going to do?"

"I said no, of course. So they threatened me. Said that I'm going to start losing things that I care about unless I change my mind."

Aurora paces around the room. Her quickened breathing matches mine.

"That's why I broke up with Harley. I don't want her anywhere near here when they come back. There may be a chance that they don't know about her."

"She's the first one they'll come for to make you pay," Aurora says as a matter of fact, as if I didn't know that already.

"Do you think there's any chance that it's

going to be okay?"

She shrugs her shoulders and looks away. She doesn't have to lie to me. We both know the truth.

"Tell me everything," she finally says.

IT'S hard to know where to begin so I just start at the beginning.

Eleven years ago.

I was young, right out of college.

I had big dreams of running a start-up. I wanted to grow my own company from the bottom up.

I knew that people at Stanford would just have their professors connect them with some venture capitalists to raise seed money for operating expenses.

I'd read about these stories online. They didn't have anything but an idea and that was enough to get started, to hire employees who would make your dream a reality. I didn't know anyone in Silicon Valley and everyone at my school was looking for internships and regular entry-level positions.

But I had bigger aspirations. I must've reached out to two hundred venture capitalists by emailing and calling them directly, all to no avail.

I did everything short of showing up on their doorstep and forcing my way inside.

Looking back, maybe I should've worked harder.

Maybe I wouldn't be in this mess otherwise.

There was a guy who raised one million dollars for a hotel idea where he would buy small cabins and place them within two hours driving distance from the city and then let people stay in them for $99 a night.

That idea wasn't some complicated tech company. It was easily executable all on its own, starting with one cabin at a time.

But instead of starting small, this guy started with ten cabins and spent most of his time raising more capital for operating expenses.

If these people would invest in something like that, then why wouldn't they invest in my e-publishing idea?

But they didn't. In fact, I never even got the chance to make a presentation because none of them ever got back to me.

10

JACKSON

TEN YEARS BEFORE...

I didn't know the right people and in the investment business, connections were everything.

Frustrated and angry, I turned to my parents for help.

They didn't have any money, but that's not what I was seeking.

I needed their advice.

After listening to me, they looked at each other for a moment and Mom started to say something.

But my dad cut her off.

"No, absolutely not."

"What?" I demanded to know. "Please tell

me. If you know anyone who could help, I need to know who they are."

But my dad was absolutely adamant about it, so I let the conversation drop for a while. Until he went to sleep. Then I found Mom in the kitchen and begged.

"I'm not looking for much. I mean, I am by regular people's standards. But VCs, they give away hundreds of thousands as if it's nothing."

"VCs?" Mom asked.

"Venture capitalists."

"This person isn't exactly that."

I waited for her to continue. "Please, you have to tell me."

I begged and begged, and eventually she caved.

She was acting against her better judgement and, now, looking back I wish more than anything that she hadn't told me a word.

She should've kept that name to herself.

Maybe then everything would be different.

"Andrew Lindell," she said the name softly, as if even uttering it out loud would stir something in the world.

"Who is he?"

"He's a bookie. He once lent your father a

hundred thousand dollars and he lost it all on three games of blackjack."

I clenched my jaw. Yes, I remembered that time. It was soon after that we moved into the RV and traveled around the country attending art fairs, shopping at yard sales, and reselling those things at flea markets.

"What happened to Dad's debt?" I asked. I knew about the gambling, but not the name of the man who lent him the money.

"We paid it all back."

"And now?"

"Now, it's all fine. Dad goes to meetings for his gambling and he hasn't been in a casino since."

Suddenly, our hushed tone conversation was interrupted by my not so much sleeping father.

He rushed into the room, yelling at Mom for ever saying that man's name again.

"Don't you remember what we've been through? Why tell him about Lindell? He's no good. His whole family is no good!"

"He was asking," Mom started to say.

"It doesn't matter! No child of mine will ever borrow a cent from that sadistic fuck. Do you know what they do to people who can't pay them? He's looking for a Goddamn business investment. What if the company goes under? How will he pay him back then?"

As my parents argued, I memorized the name, branding it on my soul.

This would be my way out.

I didn't care about the danger. I was naive. Stupid. Ignorant. But mostly, I was too in love with my own idea to know how foolish I was being.

AFTER SOME MORE PESTERING and a promise that I would only pursue this if it felt safe, Mom finally caved and told me where to find him.

He was at a pool hall not far from our house in Tucson, Arizona.

I went there to scope it out and quickly found him in the back with a group of bodyguards crowding around.

Apparently, he owned the place and no one could see him unless they were exclusively invited.

At first, they didn't want to let me through,

but when I mentioned my father, they finally waved me through.

Andrew Lindell was a short man with thick dark hair and glasses. The glasses caught me off guard.

I had imagined him to be a thug, some punk in a leather jacket and muscles that were bigger than his brain.

But this man looked like an accountant.

He even played pool like one. He wasn't very good, but everyone he played with cheered him on anyway.

When we spoke, he told me how much he missed working with my father but mentioned nothing about his once overdue debts.

I decided not to bring it up either.

When he finally asked me what I wanted, I launched into my proposal.

"I have this idea of an online publishing business. Amazon has just come out with its Kindle and everyone will be reading eBooks very soon. People will probably read more eBooks in the future than real books."

The more I talked about books and online publishing, the more glazed over his gaze became.

He didn't seem to know one thing about what I was talking about, but I kept talking anyway.

"So, what is your idea exactly?"

"We will publish books. We will be a publishing company, but we'll specialize in the online space. We'll find writers who are looking for someone to publish their work, edit it, and publish it."

He nodded slowly. "Why?"

"To make money. We'll focus on popular genres like romance, fantasy, science fiction, young adult. The things that people are writing on their own and publishing online. And we'll just reach out to them and publish their work."

"And how do you intend to make a profit?"

"We'll publish it to Amazon. They are really open to new writers now. They want people to publish on their own. And they'll pay us."

Nodding for a bit, he took the cigar out of his mouth and asked, "How much money do you need?"

"Fifty thousand."

He nodded again.

Perhaps, I asked for too much?

I only needed twenty-five, or maybe even less, but this was a man with big pockets and maybe if I had asked for more, then he would have given it to me.

"And when will you pay me back?" he asked after a moment.

"Well, you see it's an investment. It's not a loan."

"I have to get my money back, son. Will I get my money back?"

"Yes, of course."

"Well, then it's not really an investment. It's more like a loan."

I trembled and nodded.

He signaled to one of the men next to him, who disappeared into the back room and then came out with an envelope.

"Here's fifty-thousand dollars with five points interest. You have two months to get it back to me. After that you'll owe me five points a week."

Points were percent interest and five percent interest for two months was the definition of loan sharking.

But that was what he was, wasn't he?

11

JACKSON

TEN YEARS BEFORE...

I held on to that money for some time without spending a dime. I spent so long trying to get it, that when it was actually in my hands, I couldn't quite figure out what to do with it.

Of course, I knew what I needed to do.

I needed to find writers who would allow me to publish their work, and for that I needed a website, contact information, and a whole bunch of other things.

I didn't have anything set up yet, and suddenly the clock was ticking.

If I had gotten the money from venture capitalists then I would've hired a website designer and an assistant to help me go through all the prospective books and make editorial decisions.

I could've done that as well, except that I only had two months. I needed a plan that would allow me to pay Lindell off in two months without losing the money.

A few days into the first week, I actually debated just giving all of it back. I wasn't my father.

I couldn't rack up thousands of dollars of gambling debts, thinking that I could just pay it all back with one lucky hand of cards.

He was always the one who lived on the edge, and he was always the one who pushed his family to the edge as well.

Growing up like that I became methodical.

I planned three steps ahead. I did all of my homework on time and I turned it in early. In my spare time, I devoured books and took notes on anything I found of interest in them.

There are things we gain from our childhoods.

One of the most important things that I had learned was how to live with very little.

My parents always struggled with money,

and we never had much. When we relocated into the RV, we downsized even more.

I hated it at first, hating them for making me give up the few things that I had. But after a while I relished the fact that everything I owned fit nicely into a small box under my bed.

I didn't buy and hoard stuff I didn't need like my brother. Instead, I came to believe that things we own end up owning us and freed myself of them.

I probably could've easily continued the life of a monk except that I wanted to get rich. It's hard to explain why exactly, but it had nothing to do with the monetary wealth of having cash.

My desire to build something that reaped real financial rewards was driven by my general need to succeed.

Dollars were nothing but points that I could acquire, and the more points I could get the better.

I stared at the cash in the envelope trying to decide what to do.

To grow a business you need to give it tender loving care and that meant that I couldn't do it under pressure from Lindell and his loan sharking business.

But just giving this money back was also not an option.

Then I would be back to where I was in the beginning. No, I needed to use this money to get more money.

Legit money.

I searched my mind for possibilities and finally decided to just put it into my personal checking account.

Doing so would mean paying taxes on it, but that was the least of my problems. Once the money was in the account, I went online and applied for a new credit card.

I had one card with about a two-thousand dollar limit and I was faithful in not spending very much on it and paying it every month to maintain good credit.

When I was asked about my annual income, I lied and said that I made a hundred and fifty-seven thousand dollars.

I was careful not to choose a nice round number to make it more believable, though I suspected that the companies expected you to inflate your salary a bit.

Later that day, I got an email saying that I was approved for a ten thousand dollar limit, and that I could increase it if I could show that I had more money in my bank account.

I had read about this as a strategy to increase your credit card limit on a few forums. I quickly submitted all the required paperwork and waited.

A week later, I received another email.

I had been approved.

My new credit card limit was forty-five thousand.

To celebrate, I did cartwheels in my parents' living room and then went back to the computer and applied for another card and did this all again.

Another week later, I had a total of eighty seven thousand dollars in credit with zero percent interest for six months.

Now, this was more like it.

Without even waiting another day, I immediately went back to Andrew Lindell and returned his money.

I also added the five percent interest that I would've owed two months later.

"But it has only been two weeks," he pointed out.

I nodded and shrugged.

"I appreciate your help and would like to pay early."

"No one pays early."

I shrugged and turned away from him.

"Where are you going?"

"I have returned your money plus some, and I'm going home now."

Lindell nodded, looking at me suspiciously.

My heart pounded out of my chest, but I continued to breathe slowly to stay calm.

I prayed that he wouldn't see the beads of sweat forming on my forehead. I decided not to wait for his permission.

I took another step away, but his bodyguards blocked me.

"Can I go now?"

He thought about it for a moment, but eventually gave his go-ahead. I let out a sigh of relief and walked away.

"How did you get the money back to me so quick?" he yelled after me.

"I decided that I didn't need it anymore."

"Yeah, right." He laughed, not believing my lie. "I'm going be checking on you, Jackson Ludlow."

12

JACKSON

NINE YEARS BEFORE...

With room to breathe, I took my time starting the online publishing company.

I worked all day and all night, but I did almost everything myself and without the pressure of paying off a big debt at the end.

Even though I had the credit, I wasn't sure when money would start coming back into the company, so I did everything myself. I learned how to make a basic but appealing website.

I reached out to writers myself and I posted announcements for the company seeking new books in various writing-related forums.

I started out with three books and then by the end of the year I had ten, across three genres.

I learned how to format them and to upload them to Amazon and other platforms, and the money started to trickle in.

The world was different then.

Now, self-publishers who want to compete in the crowded space need to learn a lot about marketing and advertising and be willing to invest some money into Facebook to grow their business.

But back then, eBooks were brand new and no one really had smartphones yet so I didn't really need to do any advertising at all to get sales.

The harder I worked, the more my sales grew. At one point I was making nine thousand dollars a month and I thought that I was rich.

For a kid who grew up with very little, the idea of making over a hundred thousand dollars a year was hard to comprehend.

Especially from a business that I made with my own two hands. I was over the moon, and then it all came crashing down.

My father was in debt again.

He was too embarrassed to borrow money from me so he went back to Lindell who lent him another hundred and fifty thousand.

He lost all but twenty of it and my mom reached to me for help.

"I don't know what you expect me to do," I said. "I don't have that kind of money."

"Yes, you do," she insisted. "Or I'm sure you can figure something out."

"Why doesn't he figure something out?" I insisted.

"He has to pay Lindell back in two days. He's out of options. He wants to go back to the casino and try to win it all back with the twenty grand that he has left. But you know how it works. When the cards know that you're desperate, things don't work out for you."

"That's not the cards, Mom. It's the nature of the game. The house always wins. How much money does he have to lose to get that?"

We went back and forth in circles to no purpose. Her only goal was to convince me to help him and mine was to convince her to stop enabling him.

"You don't know what Lindell is capable of."

I rolled my eyes. "He owns a pool hall in Tucson. How bad can he be?" I asked a bit too confidently. It didn't take me long to forget how much terror he inspired in me not too long ago.

Mom shook her head and started to cry. My heart warmed up and I put my arm around her.

"Andrew Lindell is the youngest son of the powerful Lindell family. He's kind of a black sheep of the family, but they are all very bad. They own a lot of real estate in New York and investments in Russia and Saudi Arabia. They are connected with all the oligarchs and the sultans and all the worst powerful people in the world. The enemies of the Lindell family tend to disappear, never to be heard from again. There are rumors that they work with CIA black sites where they torture people outside of the United States but with the sanction of the CIA."

My heart sunk. I was scared of Lindell when I thought that he was just a local gangster, let alone someone who is connected so far and wide.

For a moment, I thought that maybe my mom was exaggerating, or flat out lying. But I have never seen her look so scared before.

"What about what you did before? The RV?" I asked.

"I'm not sure if he will be so receptive to getting the money back after a year like he was before. Something is different now. He is always telling your father how he regretted not making you pay him more money back."

My body tensed up.

"He knows that you are doing well now."

"How?"

"He has access to lawyers and investigators. I don't know. But you have to help him, Jack."

"And then what? I give him the money, lose everything that I have built and he goes back and gambles it all away again."

"He's going to go back to meetings. He's not going to do this again," Mom promised even though we both knew it was a lie.

I took the evening to think about it.

I got angry, even put my fist through the wall, but eventually figured out a way to come up with the money.

My father contributed the twenty grand that he had and paid the rest of his debt to Lindell with my money.

My credit cards were maxed out and I borrowed money from what I owed my writers.

I promised to pay them back, but months passed and I couldn't. I didn't have any more credit to extend and they were getting upset.

Within a few months, almost all of them left

and the only thing I could do was to declare bankruptcy.

And still, my ties to the Lindell family weren't over.

Every few years, my father would stop painting and going to Gamblers Anonymous meetings and would find himself in the casino.

Every couple of years, I would again hear from my mom about his debts and I would again be forced to pay.

I knew that I was paying into a vicious cycle but I couldn't see my way out of it. That was, until I started to make real money.

Then the occasional hundred grand didn't matter anymore and I cut off all ties with them otherwise.

13

JACKSON

PRESENT DAY...

Harley doesn't know about any of this. To her, my parents are just quirky artists who live in Barcelona.

They are those people, too, but there's this other part of them.

I didn't tell her any of this because some histories are just too painful to go into. I wanted to forget and I thought that I could.

I haven't heard from Andrew Lindell in a long time and I had almost forgotten about him.

When I tell Aurora the whole story, she listens carefully nodding her head. She knows bits and pieces of it from the past, from when we were first together, but this time I tell her everything.

Someone has to know just in case... something happens.

"I don't know what to say to you, Jackson. This is really bad. So, what happened that day when you broke up with Harley?"

I take a deep breath, fighting back tears. It had to be done, I say to myself silently. You didn't have a choice. You had to protect her. I know all of these things, but that doesn't make me miss her any less.

"Someone stopped me on the street. Martin and the other bodyguards crowded around me, but he said he was just the messenger. He said that Andrew Lindell wants another meeting."

"Why did you go?"

"I didn't think I would at first. But then I wanted to find out what he wants. My debts have been paid plus some."

"So, you went?" Aurora asks.

I nod. I don't know what would've happened if I hadn't, but ignoring the Lindells has generally not been a good idea.

"We met at a restaurant for lunch. It was crowded and there were kids running around everywhere. You wouldn't think that it would be at a place like that where my life would change forever."

Aurora shakes her head.

"He looked different actually. He has a five-hundred dollar haircut, no glasses, impeccably tailored suit. Even a briefcase. Apparently, he has been made Chief Operating Officer of Lindell Industries. They have expanded into microprocessors and other tech as well as more real estate here and abroad."

"They have properties all over Europe," Aurora confirms. "They even own a couple of banks in Cyprus and Italy."

I don't want to dance around the point much longer. I've been talking long enough about everything but what's really on my mind.

"He wants half of my company."

She stares at me.

"What do you mean?"

"The Lindell family and their holdings want to invest in Minetta and in return they want a fifty percent share."

"That means, they want controlling interest."

"Yes."

We stand and look at each other, each processing what this means on our own. For me, this means that I will no longer be the owner and even if I stay on as the CEO, they can fire me at any moment.

I currently own seventy percent of the company and Aurora owns the other thirty.

If they want half then we will have to split the other fifty percent.

But worse than that, we'll have to work with them.

"Why do you think they want this? Don't they know that we're losing money and it's not actually doing that well?"

I think about that for a moment.

"I think that's precisely why they want it."

She furrows her brows.

"They are involved with a lot of shady people. And those people need to launder their money in order to make it clean. Especially the Russians. So they sell them properties at cheaper prices, they flood into the United States, the UK, and Europe and fill it with empty mansions that they own but don't live in."

"So they want Minetta to launder money through it?"

"I don't know exactly but I'm sure that having the credit that Minetta has will go a long way toward helping them achieve their illegal goals. I've read somewhere that for every legitimate company that the Lindells have, they also own five shell corporations. No one knows the extent of their corruption."

Aurora makes us some food and then asks me what else happened at lunch.

Now, we're getting to the hard part.

"I said that I wasn't interested. So Andrew told me I could either be open to talking to him in a professional way or he could make things very difficult for me. He mentioned that he knows that I have a girl that I'm interested in and he made threats against her."

Aurora shakes her head.

"'I wouldn't want anything bad to happen to her,' he said."

"What did you say?"

"I denied it. I acted as if his information was wrong and I got the feeling that he believed me. But in order to make sure he did, I needed to break up with her. If they knew that there was someone I cared about that much, she would be their first target."

"You did the right thing, Jackson."

"Yeah? So, why do I feel so shitty about it?"

We eat in silence, lost in our own thoughts.

I know that Martin will take good care of Harley, but I hate the fact that I had to break her heart.

For a moment, I consider the possibility of reaching out to her and telling her the truth.

I want to do this so badly, but I can't. If she knew the truth, even a kernel of it, then her life might be in danger again.

The only way the Lindells will leave her alone is if they believe that she has nothing to do with this on any level.

So the only way for her to be safe is for us to be apart and for her to believe that I don't love her.

I don't want to talk about this anymore, so I head back upstairs. I want to be alone to figure things out, but my thoughts start to jumble around in my head.

The Lindells have made a threat against Harley and now that I don't have her, they'll probably threaten someone else.

I need to come up with some sort of plan. But nothing comes to mind.

14

HARLEY

WHEN DARKNESS DESCENDS...

Days turn into weeks and darkness settles in around me, wrapping around me like a forgotten blanket.

It's comfortable to lose myself in this world. I stream shows for hours each day and I never turn off the TV.

Being alone with my thoughts feels like the worst thing in the world, so I do anything to fill the void. It's nice to have other people to listen to. It's nice to have other people talking about their problems.

At least, they're not my problems.

Julie has stopped trying to rouse me and invited Martin inside.

I didn't want him here, but she felt too bad

for him standing outside the door during his shifts. When he sleeps, another guard comes to stay with us.

I don't know his name because I never bothered to ask. I don't care. I don't want to meet new people.

I don't want to make nice.

I don't want to be friendly.

Everything seems too difficult.

Even taking a shower seems like a task that is just too insurmountable.

I hear them somewhere in the background.

Laughing.

Talking.

I turn to face them.

I see them smiling.

She reaches for his hand and he touches her back.

They are flirting.

How can they be doing that when I'm going through this?

Julie and Martin are only a room away from me and I feel like they are on the screen. They aren't really here and they aren't really real.

MORE TIME PASSES, but everything stays the same. Jackson is gone and I'm all alone. I will never meet a man like him again.

I don't even want to. This is what it's going to be like for the rest of my life. Oily stringy hair.

I don't even have enough energy to blot it with dry shampoo. Dry skin. Brittle nails.

Clumpy mascara on my eyelashes.

I never bothered to fully wash it off when I first came home. Later, I said to myself.

Later, I'll feel better and that's when I'll do it. But I didn't. Later, I felt worse than I did originally. Later made everything feel like crap.

JULIE AND MARTIN are seeing each other now.

They spend all of their time talking to each other, making boring jokes.

They touch each other's faces now, but they haven't had sex.

At least, not here. Did they sleep together already? I have no way of knowing. It would require me to talk to them again in something other than grunts.

She continues to bring me food and water, but she's getting frustrated.

I don't eat much but I drink plenty. The only time I get out of bed is to go to the bathroom to relieve my bladder.

I wait until I can't wait anymore and I feel like I'm about to burst. That's the only thing that feels good nowadays.

I've watched so many shows that my head spins and the headache from all of the chatter and the flickering of the screen is getting to be too much.

I've SPENT days making plans for tomorrow. I'll get up and do something productive tomorrow.

Tomorrow will be a new day.

But the day would come and pass and I wouldn't do what I promised. And then suddenly, this afternoon, something feels different.

I turn off the screen and just get up.

No plans.

No promises.

No lies.

I get out of bed, and instead of going to the bathroom, I go to the kitchen and make myself something to eat.

Martin and Julie are sitting on her bed, but they don't utter a word. I feel their eyes peering into the back of my head and I know that they're mesmerized.

That's okay. I'm not doing this for them.

I ignore them and make a sandwich. After chowing it down in four bites, I go to the bathroom and close the door.

I turn on the water and lather my hair. Warm soothing liquid running down my naked body makes me come alive.

Every pore suddenly opens up as my eyes close. The water rushes down my forehead, eyelids, and all the way down to the floor.

It consumes me, washing away my old self. I want to stay here forever. I stay until the heat runs out.

I don't want to put my old dirty clothes back on so I wrap myself up in the towel. My hair gets wrapped in another towel.

I look at myself in the mirror.

My eyes are circled with blackness.

I look tired, but awake. I don't linger long. I

head straight to my closet and find fresh clothes to wear.

Martin and Julie are so surprised that they barely look away in time before I take the towel off and change. I see him turn his face away and hear him whisper, "I'm not looking."

They are comfortable with each other. They hold hands. They lean on each other as they stand. They kiss on the cheek.

When I turn around to face them, I realize that this is the first time that I have ever looked at Martin, really saw him.

He is in his late twenties, thin but fit. He has a chiseled body and kind eyes. His shirt is a bit too tight.

He wants people to notice his body and most do.

His hair is shaggy, probably specifically cut to look disheveled.

"How are you feeling?" Julie asks slowly. I can sense her fear.

She's afraid of doing or saying anything that will make me retreat back into my cocoon.

But she shouldn't be.

I have no plans to go back there.

"Better."

"Good. Good." She gives me a hug.

"I'm going to go outside," I announce after I break myself free of her.

Martin hesitates.

I know he needs to come with me and I'm in no mood to fight him.

I put on my coat and hat and gloves and boots. Still he hesitates, whispering something to Julie.

He's not really this unsure.

She's the one who has made him this way.

Or maybe it's her uncertainty that's brushing off on him.

Or maybe he just defers to her because she's my roommate.

I don't know. I don't care.

"Martin has to come with you," she says, bracing herself for my response.

"I know. That's why I told you."

15

HARLEY

WRAPPED IN GRAY...

They follow after me. I can sense their whispers.

They are analyzing me.

Studying me.

Trying to figure me out.

There is nothing to figure out. I am just a broken woman on a walk. That's all I am. There's no mystery here.

You wouldn't think that it's possible to start life over with a crack in your heart, but life is full of impossibilities.

The only thing that tortures me now is why.

Why did he do this to us?

Why did he make me believe in a fairy tale and then snatch it away?

Why? Why? Why?

A million times why?

The further I walk, the closer I seem to get to my pain. It surrounds me. It wraps me up like a big warm blanket, refusing to let me go.

I want to fight it.

I want to pull away, but I don't have the strength.

At least, not in my mind.

My body has other plans.

My feet keep taking one step after another.

My hands keep burying further inside of my coat.

My skin keeps getting colder and colder in the frost.

"Do you know why he did this?" I ask Martin. They are both surprised, not so much by my question but by the fact that I am even talking to them.

"No, I don't." He shakes his head. I stop and examine his facial expression. It's blank. But perhaps it is always like that. I do not know him well enough to make a decision one way or another. So, I have to be satisfied with whatever he says. I am not.

"You have to tell me the truth. It's not going to

change anything, but it's going to make me feel better."

Julie squeezes his arm. He looks at her and then at me. We both wait.

"I don't know anything," he says, sticking to his story. I ball up my fists with anger, but I am too cold to take them out and throw a punch.

WE ARE NOW WALKING in unison, all three of us across the pavement in a row, like an obnoxious group of tourists.

Julie and Martin talk among themselves.

They hold hands.

They snuggle up against each other and brace themselves against the wind. I take a step away from them, keeping my distance.

I don't want their love to rub off on me.

I don't want to feel worse, though that hardly seems possible.

Staying next to them is necessary.

I couldn't walk in front of them much longer. It reminded me too much of Parker. They were right behind me, watching me.

Observing me.

Stalking me.

Now, being next to them, it feels normal. Like we are just a normal group, friends, even. But inside, I feel anything but normal. I doubt that I'll ever feel normal again.

WHEN I GET HOME, I open my computer for the first time since it happened. Much to my surprise, and perhaps dismay, the world did not stop turning. In fact, people continued to buy my books.

I sold almost four hundred copies.

I stare at the number.

It doesn't quite make sense.

Can this be real?

Did three-hundred and eighty-four people really buy my book?

I click on the Facebook Ads Manager.

The cost per click is around twenty-five cents, which is pretty good. People are clicking and buying my books.

I make some more images and start new ads. This process doesn't take me long anymore. I've been somewhat of an expert. I have a system and I know exactly what I need to do. The only thing that takes time are the images and the copy.

How absurd is it to look up images of sexy guys to sell people on the idea of love when that's the last thing that I'm feeling right now?

As I work, my mind becomes occupied and suddenly the pain that was consuming me loosens its hold.

It no longer feels like an invisible hand is strangling me. It's just holding onto my throat, lightly.

I breathe a little easier and I continue to work.

When I'm finished with the marketing and advertising aspect of the business, I open the document that I was last working on.

There are notes below for what's to come in the next chapters. I read them and the story seems completely foreign to me.

Like someone else wrote it. More than that actually. It's as if it were written in another language altogether.

I can't possibly write when I'm feeling like this, I decide.

But my fingers touch the keyboard and my

mind, thirsty for something other than sorrow, starts to form words.

A few words form a sentence and one sentence follows another. Quickly, I am transported to another world and I am not so consumed by the troubles of this one. Occasionally, I glance over at Martin and Julie.

They eat dinner.

I write.

They do the dishes and have dessert.

I write.

They climb into bed and wrap themselves with a big comforter.

I write.

With each page that I write, the grip around my throat loosens more and more and finally I can take a full breath again.

16

JACKSON

WRAPPED IN GRAY...

Everything is a blur of a blur of a blur. I work but it's more like pretending to work. What I'm really doing is waiting.

I'm waiting for them to make their move. They made their threat, I walked away and now it's up to them.

I want to do something other than wait, but I don't know what.

As days pass, I lose myself in oblivion.

My security team keeps telling me that everything will be alright, but I don't believe them. I know that something is about to happen, the only problem is that I don't know what.

Will they threaten my family again?

Will they threaten someone else?

How far are they willing to take things?

What will they do to make me believe them?

And then, of course, there's that off chance that it might be okay. They might not push me any further.

They have threatened me once and once I declined, they might give up.

There's a chance that might happen, right? Or am I just hoping for the impossible?

I FIND their bodies on the sidewalk, right outside my door. It's a week after I met with him for lunch.

Seven days after I told him no.

He does not make any further requests or contact. Instead, I walk out of the door and find two of my bodyguards shot dead on the street.

Their lifeless bodies lie on the pavement, dark circles of blood pooling underneath them.

The police are on their way.

A crowd of onlookers is gathering. Everyone is pointing fingers and gasping.

I just freeze in place and stare.

They are both lying face down, shot in the

back of the head. They never saw their assassins coming. But I did.

This is all my fault.

Now, two people are dead because of me. I should have known. No, I knew. This was the only thing that was going to happen. When the Lindell family wants something, they get it.

Now, I'm going to have to sell half of my business to the bastards who killed my friends.

These men have eaten breakfast, lunch, and dinner in my home for weeks. They told me about their wives and girlfriends.

They told me about their favorite places to fish and fuck.

I knew things about them others don't know about their best friends and now they are dead.

Fuck you, Andrew Lindell! I want to scream at the top of my lungs. Fuck you!

But people are watching.

The cops arrive.

They ask questions. Interview people. Interrogate me. I invite them inside and tell them as much as I can.

I don't know much. I'm sure that the man they hired is a hired gun, a professional hitman.

A ghost.

There's no point in telling the police about the Lindell's request or threats because their officials will not be able to prove anything anyway.

If the FBI can't stop them and the CIA is working with them, what hope does the New York Police Department have?

They take me down to the precinct and I again tell them about Parker. Other detectives are brought in to review the case.

They suspect that it was him who killed them even though he has no history of murder. I'm tempted to tell them more.

I want to explain. I want to share.

But I bite my tongue to keep my mouth shut. Keep quiet unless you want more people bleeding on the sidewalk.

When I finally get home, the following day, more bad news.

I THINK that she went home to Woodward, her future ex-boyfriend, but then I get a call. I'm too tired to pick up, but her name keeps flashing on my screen and I finally answer.

"Jackson? Jackson!" she shrieks into the phone and then someone takes it away from her.

"Aurora?" I call for her. My heart rate speeds up. She is the unflappable one. She is the one who can laugh off anything. I've never heard her this...distressed.

"What's going on? Where are you?"

She doesn't answer.

"Aurora!" I yell again and shake the phone, as if that is going to make her come back. "Where are you?"

"She's fine," a male voice says. It's low and menacing and has a slight thick accent, but I don't quite recognize its origin.

My phone makes a dinging noise and I glance at the screen. A request to video chat. I press on the accept button.

The first thing I see is Aurora's eyes. Wild and crazy, they are practically bugging out of her head. There's a gag around her mouth, spreading her lips apart. She can't talk but she makes a horrific, screeching noise.

"Aurora has not been a very good girl," the man says, petting her arm. "She has been lying to us."

I don't want to know what that means and I'm too afraid to ask.

"Let her go! Now!"

I hear the man laugh in the background.

My body begins to shake. I fold my arms across my chest to warm up, but it's pointless.

The cold is coming from somewhere deep within me.

"You have to let her go."

"Do we, really?" He pulls on the gag in her mouth and her head jerks backward. I reach out to help her, but she's on the other side of the screen.

How did this happen? Wasn't Woodward supposed to protect you? What happened to your security? My mind swirls around the regrets instead of focusing on the future.

The man on the other side of the phone snaps me back into the present.

"If you want this pretty woman back in one piece, you better do everything I say."

I nod and wait.

"Minetta no longer belongs to you. Let Lindell Industries pay you a very reasonable amount for a fifty-one percent share and your wife will be returned to you unharmed."

"Fifty-one percent? Andrew said he wanted fifty."

"Now, he no longer trusts you. Now, he wants a controlling share."

"I can't..." I start to say.

"You better think about it before you finish that sentence, son. The Lindells aren't fucking around. The attorneys from both sides will be arriving at your home in ten minutes. They will bring all the necessary paperwork for you to sign."

"And...if I don't?"

Aurora gasps.

"She'll have the same fate as your security team. You remember what happened to them, don't you?"

17

JACKSON

WHEN I HAVE TO MAKE A DECISION...

I can't trust him, but I can't afford to not trust him either. He has Aurora. I couldn't live knowing that I could've saved her and didn't.

The next ten minutes pass in a blink.

Before I can make a decision one way or another, four attorneys arrive at my front door.

They introduce themselves and we shake hands. They are all dressed in nearly identical black suits, which they wear like their armor. They each carry a dark suitcase with gold buckles and they quickly spread out their papers around my dining room table.

Knowing what I know about attorneys and business meetings, I know that they are expecting me to provide them with coffee and bagels. I just sit down at the head of the table and wait.

The attorneys who are supposedly on my side briefly hand me the paperwork to look over.

There are pages and pages and I go through each one carefully.

I am used to reading legalities, and this looks to be in order and up to the standards except, of course, that I will be signing it under duress.

"And if I want to take this document to my own attorneys back at Minetta?" I ask. All four of them stare at me for a moment.

"That is not really an option here, Mr. Ludlow," one of the attorneys assigned to me says. "I am sure that you are aware of the situation that your ex-wife is in at this moment."

So, this is the guy who is supposedly on my side. I wonder what the other guy is going to say, I think to myself sarcastically.

I don't need to take it to Minetta to know their response.

They will freak out.

Giving away fifty-one percent of the company means that it's no longer in my control. It means that the Lindells can do whatever they want with it in the future.

My attorneys hand me additional paperwork that I have to sign first. It's the official contract saying that they are representing me.

With a heavy hand, I pick up the pen and sign it. What other choice do I have?

As I watch my signature dry, I try to come up with one possible alternative to the scenario that they have presented with me.

What if I don't go through with this?

What if I call them on their bluff?

One of the lawyers on the other side pushes the main contract toward me. There are five places to sign at the bottom of each page and a number of additional places to initial. It's about double the size of a traditional real estate contract and I pick up the pen and begin.

When it's time for me to sign the second page, I hesitate again.

Some wealthy families have a policy.

They never pay ransom requests. It comes from the philosophy that the US government follows.

The government also never pays ransoms for kidnapped officials. They believe that by paying for ransom requests they will just encourage more people to kidnap their officials and employees.

I once had a meeting with a security team about Lila when she was just born urging me to agree to the same terms.

Apparently, kids of the wealthy are often at risk of being taken. I worried about this for a while after I signed that policy, wondering if I could actually go through with it if someone had taken her.

It's one thing to put your name on a piece of paper and it's a whole other thing to actually go through with it.

But after her death, I haven't given anything like this anymore thought.

Until today, that is.

The fear in Aurora's eyes comes back to me. I should've sent Aurora away just like I had sent Harley away.

The reason they took her is that she was someone near me who they could take. Everything that happened to her is my fault and now it's up to me to save her.

I know what the Lindells are capable of and I am certain that they will take out their anger on her.

She may be married to a royal in Europe, but that won't matter.

They'll just make her disappear and no one will ever hear from her again.

I put my initials in every space and sign and date the bottom of every page until I get to the last spot. This will seal the deal. I lift the pen from the paper and wait.

"I need more time," I finally say.

"You do not have more time," the lawyer from the other side says.

"You are almost there. Just one more signature and it's all over," my lawyer says.

What if I were to sign this and then argue that it was all done under duress in court?

That's possible, right?

It will be a long drawn out legal battle, but maybe then I can get my company back and free Aurora.

Usually, duress is really hard to argue unless they actually have a gun to your head, but this will qualify.

They are making me choose between my company and saving someone's life. It's not really signing a contract willingly, or with a free and clear mind.

"Mr. Ludlow, please sign at the bottom," one of them says. I take a deep breath.

"Mr. Ludlow, you do not want to make the situation worse. Mr. Lindell wants to have a good working relationship with you."

I roll my eyes and laugh.

"Are you kidding me?"

"He made you a fair offer before, but you turned him down. Then he was forced to take things to the next level."

"Forced to?" I shake my head. "I didn't force him to do anything. Has he ever considered just taking a no and moving on?"

"No, he hasn't. Mr. Lindell doesn't accept no for an answer."

I shake my head. "That's because he's an arrogant bully who only thinks about himself."

"You are, of course, entitled to your opinion, but that does not change your current predicament. We have authorization to show you this video if you choose not to sign the contract."

18

JACKSON

WHEN I WATCH THE VIDEO ...

My heart sinks.

He pulls out his phone and turns the screen toward me.

It's Harley.

She's walking toward her building with a bag of groceries. Martin, her bodyguard, is following closely behind.

Suddenly, something else starts to creep onto the screen from the bottom. It's long, black, and made of metal.

As the camera pans, I see the 9mm handgun in the assassin's hand.

He's standing only a few feet away from them. This is exactly how my bodyguards were murdered.

A stranger walked up to them and shot them in the back of their heads.

I clench my fists as my whole body tenses up. A mixture of anger, regret, and despair courses through me.

I tried to protect her but they were one step ahead of me. I should've never broken up with her, I should've taken her somewhere far away from here like she wanted.

I should've listened to her and then things might have been okay. But they're not.

I pick up the pen and sign on the last line.

Nothing matters anymore.

I don't care that I don't own Minetta.

I don't care about going to court and making a case for duress. All I want is for Harley to be safe.

"Great, thank you very much," the lawyer with the video says. "Now, if you do not mind, I'm going to turn the camera toward you and record a little video of you."

"What kind of video?" I ask, despondently.

"We would like you to just make a statement that you have made this agreement with Lindell industries without duress and this is really what you think is best for your company."

The absurdity of this statement makes me chuckle.

"How will anyone ever believe that?" I ask. "I mean, why in the world would I want to just give him fifty-one percent of the company?"

"Oh, of course, I'm sorry. I forgot to give you this."

I stare at the check that he hands me. It's printed from Lindell Industries and addressed to Minetta. The memo line reads, *In exchange for a fifty-one percent share*. I resist looking at the amount until I can't not look anymore.

"He is giving me a check for fifty-million dollars?"

"Of course." The lawyer chuckles. "How else could this deal go through?"

"And, of course, we will accompany you to the bank to see that you deposit it in the account."

A wave of relief sweeps over my body. It's not that I'm actually relieved, it's just that my body is giving up.

The Lindells have thought of everything. Of course, the contract would mean nothing if they didn't pay me for the share.

But they didn't actually pay me what it's actually worth.

They paid me a lot more of its value. There are many different ways to estimate the worth of a company but given how much money it has been losing recently, it's definitely not worth fifty-million.

When I made the deal with Aurora, she paid me two million in exchange for thirty percent. That was more of an accurate estimate of Minetta's worth.

"This is way too much," I point out.

"Yes, the Lindells are aware of that, of course. But they know that you are giving away the controlling interest of the company and they want to compensate you adequately for it," the other lawyer from the opposing side says.

Yeah, right, I say to myself.

No, what they're really doing is paying me extra because they are going to turn Minetta into a company for laundering money.

It's the same reason why all those oligarchs overpay for real estate in New York. They don't care how much it is, they just need to find a way to launder their billions.

Each one of them carefully goes over the

paperwork that I signed, making sure there's not a single mistake.

Then they close their briefcases and collect their things.

"I'll deposit this later today," I say as casually as possible. Maybe if they see me cooperating then they'll let me off the hook.

"No, I'm sorry," one of my attorneys says. "We have to follow the protocol exactly. We will accompany you to the bank, deposit this into the account, and once we know that the amount has cleared then you will be free to go."

He may be my attorney on paper, but he has none of my best interests in mind. He sounds like he is one of the kidnappers, forcing me to pay a ransom in exchange for Aurora. The only difference is that instead of money, they want my company.

"How will I know that Aurora will be fine?"

"She is fine. She will be let out as soon as the money clears your account."

"Is that your policy with all of your hostages?"

"Mr. Ludlow, there must be some sort of misunderstanding. Lindell Industries does not take hostages."

I laugh, shaking my head. He must be delusional.

"So, how do you explain this situation?" I ask. "With Aurora?"

"That was just a negotiating tactic."

He's so full of shit that he actually believes his lies.

WHEN WE GET to the main bank, we go straight to the back room and meet with the bank manager and his advisors.

This is one of the oldest buildings in New York. Its tall ceilings and almost gothic architecture with stained windows and elaborate banisters gives the place gravitas and significance.

But none of these things change the fact that they are helping the Lindells commit massive fraud.

I sign the back of the check and the manager processes the transaction.

"How long will it take to clear?"

"Usually two to three days, but given the special circumstances of this transaction, they will be available in your account in a few minutes, Mr. Ludlow."

Perfect, I say to myself sarcastically. How convenient.

Of course, all of this could've been done with a wire transfer, by just wiring the money from his account to mine without me being here at the bank.

But I have the feeling that the Lindells wanted to make sure that people saw me. Wire transfers are done electronically but checking account deposits of this amount require the person's actual presence.

They wanted me to actually come here, in person, sign the back of the check, and go through the motions.

Everything is recorded, only further solidifying their case that the company is now theirs and that this transaction is not conducted under duress.

They may be many things but they are not dumb.

19
___

JACKSON

WHEN THEY LEAVE ME ALONE...

After we walk out of the bank, the lawyers all pile into the same town car and disappear down the street.

They offered to give me a ride back to my house, but I said no. I do not want to spend any more time with them than absolutely necessary.

I try to process the moment as it is now. I am no longer the main shareholder of Minetta, and that means that I have no say in what they are going to do with the company.

A part of me wishes that they just took the whole thing away from me. What's the point of holding on to what's left?

The contract that I signed keeps me at CEO, but it's not really the job I want.

I built that place from scratch and to keep running after this coup just seems pointless.

Companies are not just these inorganic objects that you can just toss to one side.

The thing that my mind keeps coming back to is the employees. Minetta is their livelihood.

It's how they pay rent and their mortgages. It's how they support their children. If I let the Lindells drive it into the ground, what happens to them?

I pull my phone out of my pocket.

I should call them, at least the department heads and let them know what's going on.

But I can't bring my fingers to press the dial. I've just lost everything that I've worked for.

If I were to call them now, then I would have to deal with the fallout.

There will be questions that I cannot answer.

And there will be others that I shouldn't answer. Besides, Aurora isn't safe yet. I will not do anything until I know that she's fine.

I pop into a small stationary store and look at all the beautiful paper products. Elaborate thank you cards, printed in Italy and Spain.

Fountain pens.

I pick up a handmade journal with an outline of flowers on the cover.

I don't know much about the paper industry, but the unlined paper inside the journal feels thick and expensive. It's not made of leather and I know that Harley would love this.

This is the store where I bought the paper for the letters that I wrote her. How can I make amends now for what I've done? A part of me thinks that I can just go to her and explain. But I know that I have hurt her, deeply. Is an explanation enough? Probably not. Still, I buy the journal for her and tuck it under my arm.

IT FEELS like I'm walking around aimlessly, but my feet seem to take me to her. Half an hour later, I'm standing on her corner, near her apartment building, and waiting. I even walk over to the intercom and stare at the buttons. Just press it, I say to myself. Just do it, already.

But something stops me. No, I'm not ready. I'm ready to see her, but I'm not ready to face her. And I'm not ready to be rejected by her.

She didn't let me up the last time, even after I

wrote her all of those letters. Why would this time be different? Why would she give me the chance to explain now?

When the front door starts to open, I run around the corner and hide behind the wall.

A few moments later, I glance out and see that it's just an older woman walking her little dog. I let out a deep sigh of relief and step away.

That's when I hear him. I recognize Martin's voice immediately even though I can't make out the words. I duck behind the wall again and wait.

Harley follows behind him. They walk out together laughing and head across the street. As I watch them getting further and further away, I still don't know what to do. Unable to decide, I just follow them. They go inside the large chain pharmacy at the corner and I walk in a few moments after.

Harley walks down the aisle, looking at products in the makeup section. I head down the one next to it. Luckily, the separations between the aisles are tall enough for me to remain safely on the other side. But they also make it impossible to see what's on the other side.

"What are you doing?" Martin surprises me. He looks back, making sure that she's not following him, and then pulls me past the pharmacy counter and into another aisle on the other side of the store.

"Nothing. I just wanted to see her."

Martin shakes his head, disapprovingly.

"You broke up with her. And this is the first day that I've seen her act like a human being again."

My heart clenches up from the pain that I must've caused her.

"It's over," I finally say. "The threat from the Lindells."

"What happened?"

"I signed over half of the company like they wanted. I don't think they will try to hurt her again."

Martin nods and then shrugs.

"I want to talk to her," I whisper. "I want to make things right again."

Martin looks down at the floor.

"What? What's wrong?"

"Nothing. It's just that she was really hurt. And if for some reason you don't think it's the perfect time to make contact then you should wait."

I nod. He's right. I don't know if Aurora is

back yet. All I know is that they got what they wanted. But is that enough? What will they want next?

"I understand," I mumble.

"Also, you have to stop following us. You're distracting me and I can't focus on the actual threats that she might be facing."

I go home without talking to Harley. If she's feeling better then that's enough for me for now. After tossing my coat on the couch, I head straight into the kitchen.

"Hey." Aurora walks up to me and wraps her arms around my neck.

20

HARLEY

WHEN I MOVE ON...

It's hard to say whether I am making progress because progress isn't really a linear process.

Some days, I feel normal again, or at least somewhat normal.

And other days, I miss Jackson so much that my whole body shakes.

This morning, I feel better. I still think about him, but when I try to put those thoughts out of my mind, I actually succeed.

Today, tears do not start to flow down my face at the thought of everything that I've been through.

Instead, I sit down at my desk and start to work.

The last thing that Jackson did was give me a

card with a lot of money on it. I wanted to cut it up into a million pieces.

Then I wanted to stomp on what's left and grind it into the sidewalk. But I did neither of those things.

I just kept it in my wallet until I felt better. And yesterday, I decided to keep it.

A part of me still thinks that maybe that was the wrong thing to do. The card was his way of making everything alright.

It was almost as if he were trying to pay me off and to write off his guilt. At least, that's what I thought about it at first.

But with time, I came to the conclusion that that's not what he was doing. I am still not entirely sure why Jackson broke up with me, but I know that he is not a cruel man.

He did not use me and he was not trying to pay me off with this money. He was just giving it to me because he wanted me to have it.

But I didn't accept it because I wanted to make him happy. I accepted it because I need it.

I am going to try to become a successful independent author and for that I need money.

The only way to compete is to have money for advertising and turning this money down means that I will again be back to working paycheck to paycheck to pay my portion of the rent.

No.

I've done that already and I'm ready to do something else. He doesn't know this yet, but I accepted the money as a loan.

I will be putting away whatever profit I manage to make toward paying him back every single cent of this.

I SPEND the day writing and working on marketing while Martin and Julie laugh and make cutesy looks at each other on the other side of the room.

I hate to admit it, but they actually make a pretty nice couple.

Unlike the asshole guys that Julie usually goes out with, Martin is grounded and down to earth.

He looks at her like he really sees her for the person that she is, rather than an object to hang off his arm.

I wish that they would just leave me alone

and go out somewhere together, but Martin is technically on the job.

He's my bodyguard and that means that he has to be with me at all times.

At first, I found his presence annoying and bothersome. But now, I'm pretty used to it.

It feels nice to have someone there watching over my back so that I don't have to. I had forgotten how timid I've become whenever I am outside.

My eyes are darting all over the street and around corners, in an effort to make sure that if Parker is around then I will see him first before he sees me.

But now, with Martin going with me, a big part of me is back to normal.

Safe. Is this how regular people feel?

Just at peace all the time?

Wow, imagine that.

I head to the kitchen for what feels like the tenth time today for yet another snack. I really need to cut down on all of this snacking, but I can't.

I'll stop eating all of this junk food tomorrow, I say to myself.

For now, I give them a brief nod and grab a

bag of chips that I purchased last night at the convenience store on the corner.

I should've never bought this.

Why can't you just have willpower like other people?

Just because Jackson broke up with you it doesn't mean that you have to stuff yourself with all of this crap and gain thirty pounds on top of it.

I stuff the chips into my mouth feverishly.

The salt, and fat, and fried potatoes send endorphins through my body, making me feel energized and happy.

At least, for the moment.

I eat about half a bag in no time and stare at what's left with disgust.

You don't need to eat the rest, I say to myself.

Just throw it away.

I toss it in the trashcan under the desk.

I try to focus on the words that I'm writing, but the harder I try not to think about the chips sitting less than a foot away from me, the more I think about that exact thing. Eventually, I give in and finish the bag.

Half an hour later, I run to the bathroom and bury my head in the toilet.

21

HARLEY

WHEN SOMETHING'S WRONG...

I continue to throw up most of the evening and well into the morning.

I feel so sick that I can barely make it back to my bed.

Julie brings me water with electrolytes to drink but I throw that up as well.

I spend the night lying on the cool tile floor, waiting for the next pang of nausea to set in and praying for death.

Surprisingly, I manage to make it until morning and things only get worse from there.

The nausea is pervasive and never-ending.

It seems like every time I move my head just a little bit, I have to empty the contents of my stomach.

"What did you eat?" Julie asks, sitting down on the bed next to me.

"Nothing," I whisper. My lips are chapped and I see spots whenever I open my eyes. She hands me a glass of water to drink but I push it away. I threw up the last few times I even had a drop of that.

"You have to drink something. You're getting dehydrated."

But I shake my head no.

"You think it's just the stomach flu?"

I shrug and turn away from her, burying my head in the pillow.

THE FOLLOWING day I am not feeling much better. I spent another horrendous night throwing up and Julie is so concerned that she wants me to go to the hospital.

The thought of traveling in a car over bumpy streets and sitting in the emergency room is unfathomable.

"It's going to cost a fortune," I mumble.

"Okay, fine. But I'm making you an appointment to see someone at the clinic tomorrow."

I want to fight her on this, but I am too weak and too tired. Plus, I am starting to get really worried. What if something is seriously wrong? What then? I've had a stomach flu before, but this seems like something much more serious than that. With all of these thoughts swirling around in my head, I turn toward the wall, pull the blanket over my head, and shut my eyes.

IN THE MORNING, Julie and Martin help me downstairs and into the waiting cab. The clinic is only three blocks away but there's no way I can make it down there on foot.

I can barely make it downstairs.

I am so weak, Martin is practically holding me up.

I keep apologizing for leaning on him so much and he keeps telling me to shut up.

When I buckle my seat belt, I pull the plastic bag that I brought from home out of my purse. This is my just-in-case barf bag, just in case I start to feel sick in the car.

The clinic is small and clean and, most

importantly, empty. Somehow, we manage to arrive on the one day that no one else in this city is ill. They take me right back to see the nurse. First, she asks me to pee into a cup and then to change into a paper gown and wait.

My body is ice cold by the time the doctor comes in. She is young and friendly and her hair is tied up in a loose ponytail.

She introduces herself as Dr. MacDowell and asks me how I'm feeling. I go over the highlights and then take a deep breath, waiting for a brief moment of nausea to pass over me without rushing to the trashcan.

Dr. MacDowell looks over my file and smiles.

"What do you think it is?" I ask.

"Harley, it seems that you are pregnant."

———

A QUIET HIGH pitch sound forms somewhere in the back of my head and increases in volume and intensity with each passing moment. I stare at her, unable to process what she just said.

A short strand of hair peeks out from behind her ear.

The pen that she keeps in the breast pocket of her uniform shifts slightly to the right.

A speck of dirt falls off her boot and onto the floor.

"Harley?" She touches my hand, bringing me back to reality. "Did you hear what I said?"

"No, this is impossible. We were really careful."

"We will need to double check with a blood test, of course, but the urine test did come back positive for pregnancy."

I shake my head again. "I don't think you heard me. I can't be pregnant. We were always really careful."

"Protection is not one hundred percent effective. Most of them are only ninety-nine percent effective."

My head starts to spin again. That familiar nauseous feeling comes over me, only this time I can't hold it back. Dr. MacDowell brings the wastebasket up to my face just in time.

"You seem to be experiencing a pretty bad case of nausea due to all the hormones that are surging through your body. I'm going to write you a prescription for Diclegis."

"What is that?" I mumble as I wipe my mouth with a tissue that she hands me.

"It's a specially formulated medication of an antihistamine and vitamin B6. What makes it really safe and particularly effective is that it releases slowly, so it should balance those hormones that are making you throw up throughout the day and night."

I nod.

"I actually have a few samples, so here, please take one now." She hands me two samples of about ten pills each. Then she pulls out her prescription pad and writes out the prescription.

"I would like the nurse to take your blood before you leave today. Then if once we confirm that you are indeed pregnant, you can go to the pharmacy and fill that."

"Thank you," I manage to say, still lost in a complete daze.

As I wait for the nurse to arrive, I look down at my stomach. Pregnant? How can I be pregnant?

22

HARLEY

WHEN I TRY TO FIGURE OUT WHAT TO DO…

I t's hard to say whether I feel significantly better after taking the Diclegis, because I still feel exhausted and not entirely myself.

But at least, I am no longer throwing up.

As I lie down on the bed after Julie and Martin get me home, I stare at the ceiling and think about what just happened.

This morning I was just a woman, dealing with a breakup.

Trying helplessly and without much success to move on with my life.

And now?

Now, I am pregnant.

They haven't confirmed it for sure yet with a blood test, but that doesn't mean that I'm not.

With the sample medication running through my system, my nausea wears off just a bit and is no longer that acute.

If this were simply a stomach flu, then the medication wouldn't work.

No, I'm pregnant.

What does this mean?

What can I do now?

Can I really have this baby?

I have no real job, no money, a dream of supporting myself entirely as a writer. And then there's that one really important aspect of this whole problem: the father of this baby broke up with me and wants nothing to do with me.

Julie sits on the edge of her bed, staring at me.

I told both of them what the doctor told me and made them promise not to tell a soul until I figure out what I'm going to do.

"Are you okay?" Julie asks.

I shake my head and look away from her.

I feel so ashamed.

I know that I didn't do anything wrong.

We used protection every time, but the fact that I am not to blame doesn't change anything.

"How could this happen?" I ask.

"Sometimes, things just don't work. Those little buggers get through."

She moves over to my bed, draping her arm around me.

"I'm going to support you no matter what you decide."

"I can't have this baby, Julie," I whisper. "I can barely support myself. What the hell am I going to do with a baby? I don't know anything about taking care of children."

"I know, honey. I don't know either."

"And what about Jackson? He broke up with me. I don't want to be connected to him for the rest of my life. And I can't just give up my life to take care of a child."

"I know," she whispers.

"I'm too young to be a mom. I have plans. This is going to derail everything."

"You don't have to have it," she says. "There are many options available."

I know.

I know all about the options.

Adoption.

Abortion.

There aren't really that many options, just two.

My thoughts return to my writing.

How will I be able to continue if I have to take care of the baby all the time? Writing is the only thing that makes me feel sane.

If I go more than a week without putting my pen to paper, or my fingers on the keyboard, I start to feel antsy. It's a craving.

Something that I just have to do. Other people are addicted to alcohol, drugs, sex. I'm addicted to writing.

When I imagine having a baby, the thing that I worry about most is not just the time.

Even though they are time-consuming and draining. It's also the money. Without this loan from Jackson, what he still thinks is a gift, I couldn't take the time to build up my self-publishing business.

But what happens if it doesn't work out?

What happens if people don't keep buying my books?

What then?

Then I'll have to go back to my freelance writing. Or worse yet. I'll have to get a proper entry level job.

Most of those start out at around thirty-eight thousand, maybe forty?

Is that enough to support a baby in one of the most expensive cities in the world?

And who's going to take care of this baby when I'm spending all of my time at work?

And how much is that person going to cost?

If I were a teenager, maybe I could be under the delusion that it will all work out somehow.

Teenagers don't think ahead too much.

They don't see the pitfalls in their future planning.

But I do.

I know how hard I had to work for the few dollars that I did make.

And I know how hard I'll have to work to support a little person who will eat up all of my time, love, and resources.

And for what?

"I know that you are running all of these negative scenarios in your head," Julie says. "All of the things that are going to cost you your life and career and everything that you worked for."

I nod.

"I am not pressuring you one way or another. I just want to add a perspective."

I wait for her to continue.

"What if it's not going to be terrible? What if in the end you get this person who loves you and who you love? You'll watch him or her grow up. They'll make you laugh, and cry sometimes. But mostly, they will fill your heart with joy."

I shrug. I've heard of that, of course, from parents. But I can't imagine myself feeling like that.

"The thing is that I never really wanted kids," I say. "I mean, I always thought that sometime in the future, maybe. You know? But it was never really a dream of mine."

"You never wanted to get married? Or have kids?" Julie asks. I take her by surprise. I guess I never really mentioned this before.

I shake my head. "I loved Aspen so much and when I lost him...I just never wanted to experience that again. Plus, I don't know much about babies or kids. I never spent much time with kids growing up. Just Aspen."

"You should, of course, do what you feel is right. But given how much you loved Aspen, I think you have a glimpse of what it would be like to love your own child."

I shake my head. No, there's no way. There's

absolutely no way I could love anyone as much as I loved Aspen.

"And what about Jackson?" Julie asks.

23

HARLEY

WHEN I CAN'T MAKE A DECISION...

I ignore her question and instead ask my own. "How the hell am I even going to afford to have this baby? I don't have insurance."

Julie shakes her head. She and I both know that is a major consideration.

"I read a few days ago that the average costs of a vaginal delivery across the nation is about sixteen thousand dollars," she says quietly.

"That means in New York, it's probably close to thirty," I add. We both inhale and exhale slowly.

"If I go through with this, I'm going to be in debt forever. I'm never going to be able to afford anything."

Julie shrugs. "What about Jackson?" she asks after a moment.

"What about him?"

"He's the father."

I shrug. "I don't know what you are getting at."

"Jackson Ludlow is the father and he is also a very wealthy man."

"You want me to ask him for money?"

"If you decide to have this baby, then he will have to support it. And I'm sure that he will be more than happy to provide for both you and the baby."

I shake my head and look down at the floor.

"What? What's wrong with that plan?"

"He dumped me. He doesn't want anything to do with me. What makes you think he'll even care?"

"Whatever his reason was for breaking up with you, you know that he is not a bad man. I don't think he will have any issues with supporting you and the baby. I mean, he did give you a hundred grand after he broke up with you."

"I'm going to return every last cent of that money," I insist.

"I know that you will. But it just shows that he didn't want you to have any hard feelings."

I clench my jaw.

I still feel ashamed for taking the money.

I probably shouldn't have, except that it was the only way that I could see making my business work.

Another person, someone with a little bit more pride, probably would've walked away.

But I had already seen an increase in book sales from the advertising and I didn't want to make that go away.

Over the years, I have made a lot of sacrifices for my family and now is the time that I no longer want to make them.

I just want to do the one thing that I can imagine myself doing. Is that so wrong?

"I will pay him back," I say again, not so much for her benefit but for my own.

WHEN JULIE GOES TO WORK, I'm suddenly alone with my thoughts again.

Martin is still here, but he's sitting at the

dining room table with his head buried in his phone.

He is giving me space, even though this place has very little of it.

I turn away from him to face the wall.

Can I really keep this baby?

I rub my stomach and try to imagine it getting bigger.

This whole thing is a mistake a million times over. I know that. But now that it's happened, I find it hard to press the rewind button.

An abortion is definitely an option, as is an adoption, but neither of those two choices seem like the right option for me.

I'm not sure why exactly except to say that I do have this feeling that sometimes the best things in life come as a surprise or a mistake.

It was a mistake that led me to knock on Jackson's door.

I could've chosen any of those houses, but something took me to his house.

It was like I was being physically pulled toward him.

So, maybe this mistake will also end up being a blessing?

I take a deep breath, and then another and another.

The more oxygen that comes into my system, the clearer my head gets.

Money is important, but it's not everything. Besides, Julie is right. I do have options.

This baby is Jackson's baby and he is not a greedy man. I don't know how he will react to the news, but I know that he will have no problems in helping me support it or paying for us entirely outright.

Perhaps, I should be too proud to take it, but I am not too prideful to turn it down if it means that I can spend my time doing something for a living that gives my whole world meaning.

As the nausea starts to disappear completely, my thinking clears up.

The desperation that I felt only a few hours ago, suddenly doesn't seem that drastic or extreme. In reality, I am very lucky.

Besides Jackson's money, there is something else that I have that many future single mothers don't.

I have the support of my parents.

They will undoubtably be surprised by the news, but I also know that this will make them very happy.

If I want to and if I let them, they will help me raise the baby as well.

They won't be able to move out to New York, of course, so if I want their help, I'll have to return back home.

I think about that for a moment.

Is that it?

Is that really the decision that I have to make now?

If I were to have this baby and keep it, then should I return back to Montana so that my parents can help me?

It only makes sense, I guess.

Montana is a much cheaper place to live than Manhattan.

Plus, with my parents taking the time to babysit, I will have more time to focus on my writing and growing my business.

But this would also mean leaving the one place I ever saw as my home.

24

JACKSON

WHEN I SEE HER AGAIN...

The Aurora that wraps her arms around me looks like she has aged two decades. Her skin is sallow, her lips are chapped, and her eyes are bewildered. I hardly recognize her.

"What happened? Are you okay?" I keep asking over and over again, but she just shakes in my arms.

So, I quit asking questions and just hold her. After a few moments, she pulls away.

"I'm sorry," she says. When I look at her face, there are tears streaming down her face. "I shouldn't have ever let them take me."

"What are you talking about? You have nothing to be sorry for."

She buries her head in her knees and sobs. I

don't know what else to do but to just put my arm around her and hold her.

"I should've fought harder. I should've stood up to them."

I shake my head. "You did the best you could, honey."

I haven't called her honey in years, but the word just slips out of my mouth.

"They killed two of my bodyguards. Just shot them in the back of their heads," I whisper. I feel her body recoil from me. I'm not telling her to scare her. I just want her to know how lucky she is. How lucky both of us are.

"This was the best thing that could've happened," I continue through her sobs. "I'm glad that there was something I could do to help you."

She looks up at me. Her eyes are wide with grief and sorrow. Her hair falls into her face and I push it out behind her ears. It's tangled and uncooperative and hasn't been washed in days.

"But you lost...everything."

"Just forty-nine percent," I joke. "Well, with your thirty percent, I'm down to nineteen percent, I guess."

Even though it's simple arithmetic, I haven't

really done the exact calculation in my head until this moment.

And it seems...staggering. In the blink of an eye, I've gone from being the sole owner to owning less than twenty percent.

It's so tragic that it almost makes me laugh.

But then I look at Aurora again. She shakes her head and looks down at the floor in shame. I put my finger under her chin and lift it back up.

"You have nothing to be sorry about. I would've given them everything just to protect you."

She brushes a tear from her cheek and then reaches back to me.

She presses her lips onto mine and opens hers.

I freeze.

Unlike the last time she kissed me, this one catches me by surprise. I take a moment before slowly sliding away from her.

"I'm sorry." She shakes her head and buries it in my shoulder.

"It's okay," I mumble, uncertain as to what to do next.

She has gone through a trauma and she's vulnerable. I don't want to hurt her feelings, but I also don't want to do anything to lead her on.

"Why did you do that?" she asks after a moment. "If you don't love me anymore, why did you agree to their terms?"

"They gave me no choice," I say. "They said that they were going to kill you. And I couldn't let them do that."

Aurora shakes her head.

"I love you. You know that, right? I mean, we have been through so much together. A part of me will always love you as a result. But I'm not *in* love with you, Aurora. And I'm not sure if I ever was."

She shrugs her shoulders.

"I'm sorry," I whisper.

She takes a deep breath and gathers herself.

She wipes her eyes and cheeks and straightens her clothes.

Then she flattens out her hair and pushes the loose strands more behind her ears.

When she looks up at me again, the lost little girl who buried herself in my arms is gone.

The woman standing before me now is confident and self-assured. I know that what may or may not have happened to her back there will never be revealed.

"I do appreciate what you have done for me, Jackson," she says after a moment. Even the tone of her voice is different now.

"I know you do."

"I know that you gave up a lot."

I nod.

"I have to tell you something," she says after a moment. She takes a breath to gather her strength while I wait.

"They really scared me. I have never been through anything like that before..."

"I know. I can't even imagine," I cut her off.

"Otherwise, I wouldn't have ever told them about her."

My heart skips a beat. Her? What is she talking about? I narrow my eyes.

"I thought that they were going to hurt me, even more than they did. They were asking me all of these questions. They knew about Harley being your girlfriend. They knew so much about you, too."

I nod, trying to process what she's getting at.

"I'm so sorry."

"What did you tell them?"

"Nothing. I mean, they already knew everything. But I guess...I confirmed it."

"So that's how they knew to go to her apartment?"

"What do you mean?"

"After they sent me a video of you, they sent me a video of someone following Harley going home."

"I didn't tell them anything about where she lived. I just told them that you two did date, but you weren't anymore. I told them that you broke up with her, but they didn't really believe it."

I shrug. I should blame her for not denying it more. I should blame her for not protecting Harley.

But I don't.

Only an ignorant bastard would think it's her fault.

Even if they didn't know about Harley at all and she told them about her, it wouldn't be her fault.

That's the thing about being held captive and being tortured.

We glamorize those people who keep their secrets despite being tortured, but that's not real life. In reality, people will say just about anything to make it stop.

They will reveal the truth.

They will lie.

They will even confess to crimes they didn't commit. All to make it stop. And that doesn't make them bad people. It just makes them human beings.

25

JACKSON

WHEN I MAKE PLANS...

The following day Aurora is feeling a lot better. It's hard to tell if it's all an act or not, but I decide to take her at her word. Over breakfast, she starts brainstorming all sorts of outlandish ideas about how I can get my company back. Most of them require an extensive legal battle.

"They paid me a lot more than what the company is worth," I say.

"So?"

"So, that's why I won't be able to get anything in court. They'll just see it as seller's remorse."

She doesn't seem to understand, so I go over the details of the deal. I have to hand it to them.

They really did think of everything. I had my attorneys present at the deal. I signed every part of the extensive contract.

I made a video saying that I agree to all the terms. And, to really solidify the agreement, they paid me a lot of money for my share.

"If they hadn't paid me anything then the deal wouldn't make sense," I explain. "Why would I give away so much of the company unless they were threatening me with a gun or threatening someone close to me? But by paying me so much and by taking me to the bank and getting me on film, signing the back of the check to accept the money...well, they made it pretty much impossible for me to take any legal action against them."

"So, what are you going to do?" she asks, shaking her head.

"Nothing."

"What do you mean?"

I shrug my shoulders.

"You're just going to give up?"

I've given this a lot of thought, but never once did I think of it as giving up. No, I'm just going to move on.

They paid me a lot of money for my share and since I don't have many options as far as getting the company back, I'm just going to move on with my life. I'm going to Harley, tell her everything, and beg for her forgiveness.

And if she accepts me back into her life, then we're going to go away for some time.

Just the two of us.

Somewhere far away from New York.

I want to go somewhere where life isn't so complicated.

I don't tell Aurora about all of these plans, but I go over the broad strokes.

"You can't just give up! You can't just leave," Aurora says. "No, that's ridiculous."

"Give up what? Minetta wasn't doing that well anymore. Expanding into products rather than just blogs and podcasts was your idea, not mine. The only reason I was doing it was to keep the company afloat. I didn't want all of those people to lose their jobs. Now, under the Lindell's leadership, they won't. They are going to poach the company and use it to launder money but they won't run it into the ground. They need to keep it alive so that they can do what they want with it on the back end."

"You can't just give up."

"It's no longer my vision. Minetta will become something I won't recognize. You and I both know that. Why should I stick around to watch it morph into this new beast?"

"Because...you started it. It was your baby."

"My baby grew up."

"What about your employees?"

"Like I said, the Lindells will not restructure the company. They are just going to use it for parts. So, I'm pretty sure that everyone will keep their jobs doing the same things they are doing now."

Aurora continues to argue with me, but I tune her out.

We are going in circles and none of this matters anymore.

Minetta is no longer my problem. In fact, I sort of want to give them the other nineteen percent and just be done with the whole thing.

———

WHEN I GET BACK to my office, I check my voice mail and emails.

There are about twenty unread messages from Avery Phillips, let alone everyone else.

I have been ignoring everyone at Minetta long enough and now it's time to deal with this again.

I don't want this situation weighing on me when I go to see Harley. I want this to be resolved completely.

Before calling her back, I take a moment to gather my thoughts. What exactly should I say to her?

How much should I explain?

How much of the truth do I reveal and how much do I hold back?

"I'm sorry that I haven't called you back," I start. "I was dealing with...a personal situation."

"Are you okay?" Phillips asks.

Her voice is detached, not as frantic as I had expected. Perhaps, she's past that emotion.

Or maybe she's just bracing for the worst.

I have no idea.

Phillips has worked for me for years, but I know very little about her. She keeps everything personal to herself and rarely asks me any personal questions in return.

Suddenly, I have an idea. What if I were to use this attribute of hers to my benefit?

"I made a decision that I wanted to share with you," I say.

"I'm listening."

"A few days ago, I made an agreement with Lindell Industries and sold them the controlling share of my interest in Minetta."

26

JACKSON

WHEN I DEAL WITH THE FALLOUT...

My voice is stern and definitive. I am stoic, showing no emotion. I wait for her to reply, but she doesn't. I don't explain further. I want to, but frankly I am not entirely sure what to say.

"Why?" Phillips asks after a moment.

"Andrew Lindell approached me and made me an offer I couldn't refuse."

At least, this part is true.

"But Lindell Industries isn't even in this kind of business. Aren't they in real estate? Why would they even want Minetta?"

"They are seeking to expand their holdings."

"You didn't think that you wanted to tell anyone about this?" she asks after a moment.

TANGLED UP IN HATE   165

"Like who?" I ask, as if I don't understand her question.

"Like me, for one. I am the Chief Operating Officer."

"Yes, you are. But I am the CEO. And, frankly, I don't owe you or anyone else an explanation about what I do with my share of the company."

She coughs a little bit to clear her throat. When she speaks again, her voice cracks and I realize that she is holding back tears.

"Can we talk in person?"

"I don't really know what else there is to talk about," I say coldly. My heart goes out to her. She doesn't know what's going on and I will not offer her any other explanation. Everyone knows about Lindell Industries, but not many people know about their back door, secret dealings with the oligarchs and the most corrupt heads of state in the world. And frankly, the less that she knows about any of this the better.

"So...what's going to happen now? I mean, to everyone's jobs."

"Your jobs are safe. They are just acquiring Minetta, they don't want anyone to stop doing anything that they were doing before."

"Really?" Phillips asks, surprised.

"Yes, that was part of the deal."

Actually, it wasn't. It's just an assumption that I'm making, but I don't want to worry her anymore for now. I am pretty certain that they won't fire anyone, what would be the point? They aren't trying to make a profit from Minetta, they are just going to use it as a front.

I am tempted to tell Phillips this, but I keep my mouth shut. If she knows then maybe she'll refuse to work there and she's a good COO. I don't want the Lindells putting in any of their own people into my company.

Phillips has more questions and I do my best to answer them. At the end of our conversation, I actually seem to put her at ease.

"I won't lie. I'm sorry that you made this decision, but I'm glad that everyone gets to keep their jobs. I don't want to go through working for a company doing layoffs ever again. It's heartbreaking."

I nod, inhaling deeply. I sure hope that my hunch about their plans is the right one.

"So, can I talk to you about some issues that we've been dealing with now?" she asks.

"Actually, there's something else I have to tell you."

I tap my foot on the floor, nervously.

"I'm going to be stepping down as CEO."

She doesn't say anything for a moment. I wait for her to respond and when she doesn't, I explain.

"It's just that with such a small share of the company, I am not sure whether it's in my best interest to keep running Minetta. I'm feeling a bit burnt out actually. I've been shouldering all of the stress for a very long time and I think I need to take some time for myself."

"So, take a vacation. Don't fucking resign from your job!"

Her words explode out of her and take me by complete surprise. I've never heard her curse, let alone raise her voice.

My phone beeps and when I look at the screen, I see that she's requesting to video chat with me. I don't want to take the call, but I can't force myself to *not* press the Accept button.

"What the hell is going on, Jackson? Is someone threatening you?"

I take a step back and pull the screen as far away from my face as possible. I don't want her to see the truth in it, but I fear that it's too late.

Phillips repeats her question.

"No...what makes you say that?" I finally say.

"Because this is insane. This came totally out of left field. What's going on?"

I shake my head. "Nothing. They just made an offer I couldn't refuse."

"This is your life. This is all you care about."

"No, it's not. They offered me a lot of money."

"You don't care about money." She laughs.

She knows me too well.

"You are the one boss I had who never checks his accounts. You see dollars as points. You want the profits to increase like any other CEO, but not because it's going to make you richer."

I take a deep breath. This was so much easier to do when she couldn't see my face.

I gather my thoughts and force a stern expression to it.

"I made up my mind, Avery. I don't need your permission to do any of this. And I don't owe you an explanation."

She hangs her head and rubs her right temple with her free hand.

"I know you don't," she says softly. "But...I just don't understand. Did something happen, with Harley?"

"No, nothing happened. Everyone is safe."

I shouldn't have said the last sentence. It piques her attention and she narrows her eyes.

"Did they threaten you? Did they threaten her?"

I don't want to go around in circles anymore. "Everything is fine...now."

"But it wasn't before?"

Despite my best efforts, I have given her enough clues. I can't part with any more than that.

"I've heard the rumors, Jackson. I know that the Lindells are a pretty shady bunch. After they went bankrupt with those casinos they owned in Atlantic City, no American banks would lend them money anymore. They owed everyone a lot of money. But they restructured and miraculously got loans from Deutsche Bank. And we all know that Deutsche Bank is the place where all the villains of the world keep their money. They have no scruples. They kept Mirodi's money safe after he was on the run for orchestrating a genocide of nearly half of his country just because they wanted him out."

"I didn't realize that you were so...informed about the Lindell situation."

"I know a lot. I know that they are not the

type of people to take no for an answer and they are known to use a lot of dark and illegal methods to get what they want."

"Uh-huh," I mumble.

"And I also know you. I know how hard you worked to grow this company, and that you wouldn't just sell it. No matter how much they offered you. Let alone, sell it to the likes of them."

I shrug my shoulders. Without really being privy to any of the details, she knows everything. I give up.

"It's a done deal, Avery. There's nothing else I can do."

27

JACKSON

WHEN I GO TO SEE HER...

I've waited long enough. I should have gone to see her sooner, but now I can't wait any longer.

I don't know why I had put this off so long except that I was afraid of what she was going to say.

I'm still afraid.

I am still not sure if she will let me explain, but I have to try.

I pull up to her building and drive around the corner looking for parking. Luckily, I find a spot only a block away.

I walk up to the intercom. She and Julie did not bother with putting their names next to the number of their apartment.

Most of the other people in the building have. I wonder if it's because of Parker.

Did they not want anyone to know that they live here? I stare at the number and take a breath before I press it. Then I wait.

No one answers.

C'mon, c'mon. Be home. Please, I say to myself over and over.

Meanwhile, I also hope that someone else comes to the front door and just lets me in. But I'm out of luck on both counts.

I call up again. This time, I stare right at the camera that's pointed at me.

Is no one really home? I ask my reflection in the glass. Or do you just not want to see me?

I press the button again and again, but again no one answers. After a few moments, I take a step back.

Perhaps, I should've called her phone first. Maybe just showing up here is too much of a first step to take. She is angry with me. I just broke up with her without much of an explanation. I have one now, but she doesn't know that.

Unsure of what to do next, I head back toward my car. I pick up my phone and call her number. It's not particularly surprising that no one answers. So, I text her.

HARLEY, please call me back. I really need to speak with you. I'm so sorry about everything.

AFTER I SEND THE TEXT, I re-read it again and realize just how desperate it comes off.

It sounds like it's coming from someone who has a lot of amends to make but isn't exactly sure where to start.

It sounds like it's coming from someone without much of an explanation.

I send another text.

I HAVE A LOT TO EXPLAIN. Please let me talk to you. I love you.

A BLACK TOWN car pulls up right next to me and the back door swings open.

"Jackson, get in," a familiar voice says. I clench my jaw.

"What do you want?" I ask.

"Get in," Andrew Lindell says. I take a step toward him to climb inside, but he motions for me to go around and get in the other way. Apparently, it's too much of an imposition for him to move over six inches.

Against my better judgement, I do what he says.

"What do you want?" I ask.

"Shut the door."

"My car is right over there."

"We're just going to drive around the block. We need to talk."

There aren't many legitimate businessmen who conduct their activities in the back of a town car. Knowing this, I shut the door and turn toward him.

"I am aware of your discretion with your staff at Minetta," he says, with a little smile on his face. "I really appreciate you keeping the details of our negotiation private."

I shrug. "I didn't think they needed to know about any of that."

"They didn't. But it shows me a lot that you also realized that. You'd be surprised by how people act in your situation."

I raise my eyebrows.

"So, you've done something like that before? Stolen someone else's company right from under their nose?"

"Stolen?! C'mon now." Andrew laughs. "You don't really believe that, do you?"

"What else would you call it?"

"I'd say if anyone got away with something that they didn't deserve it would be. *you*, my friend."

Andrew Lindell is one of those people who tends to rely on terms of endearment as expressions of power.

"How's that?" I ask.

"I paid you a lot more for your company than it was worth, remember?"

"Oh, yes, of course, how could I forget?"

Andrew leans in closer to me and gives me a little wink.

"Okay, let's be serious now. I like you. A lot. I always liked you. I knew that you were going to go far even back then when I first gave you that money. When you had nothing."

"I am in no mood for listening to empty compliments, Andrew. Excuse me, sir, can you please take me back to where you picked me up,"

I say to the driver. He doesn't respond until Andrew gives him a nod.

"If you don't want to be friendly, I'll respect that," Andrew says confidently. "But I did come here to talk to you about something important."

"What?"

"My sources tell me that you are thinking of resigning as CEO?"

I shrug. "Yeah, so what?"

"That was not part of the deal, Jackson."

"What are you talking about? I own less than twenty percent of the company."

"Be that as it may, you will continue to stay on as its head."

"You're not going to let me quit my job?"

"It is very important that everything continues at Minetta as it was when you were the owner. We don't see a reason to create any waves or unnecessary drama."

"But I don't want to keep working there."

"That, frankly, doesn't really matter. You will continue in your position...indefinitely."

I laugh and reach for the door. How could he say that? I mean, he can't just keep me employed in a job I don't want to have or need to have.

Andrew puts his hand on my shoulder.

"You will continue in your position as CEO of Minetta Media for as long as I say." His words are slow and deliberate. "Otherwise, I will fire every single person there and replace them with my own people."

My heart sinks. I turn around to face him. I meet his dead eyes straight on and wait.

"I know that you do not want that to happen," he says, this time with a smile at the corner of his lips. "So why don't you just make it easier on everyone and stay on in your current position? You will, of course, be handsomely compensated."

28

HARLEY

WHEN I SEE HIM...

"Who is that?" I ask, walking up to the monitor near the front door.

Someone has been ringing the doorbell non-stop.

We rarely get any unannounced visitors, let alone ones that are that insistent.

For a moment, I think that it's Julie and she just forgot her keys.

But the expression on Martin's face tells me that it's probably not.

I walk over to the camera and stare at his face. Jackson is looking up at me, his eyes are pleading.

"Harley, let me in," he says. "Please."

His words startle me.

A moment ago, I was safe in my home. I have cooped myself away from him and all the pain that he has caused me.

And now, suddenly, he has invaded my space.

He's not here, yet he is. With only a few words, my whole being yearns for him again.

"I don't want him here," I say to Martin and turn to walk away. But the problem is that I only turn in my mind.

My body remains fixed in place, staring at him.

It's as if those piercing eyes have put a spell on me.

I can't make myself move an inch.

"Are you sure?" Martin second-guesses me. I know that he's doing it because I can't pull myself away from the screen, but it irks me nevertheless.

"I don't want him here," I say sternly.

This time the words come out with a lot more determination and confidence. This time, I bring myself to look away from him and finally walk away.

He calls again and again until Martin puts

the buzzer on silent. He sits down next to me on the couch.

He's a stranger that I have been forced to get to know over the last bit of time and I wish that it were Julie sitting next to me instead of her boyfriend.

"Are you okay?" he asks after a moment. I shrug.

"I am here if you want to talk."

I shrug again. "Isn't that a bit outside of your job description?"

"Not really." He shakes his head.

I furrow my brow.

"I'm in the protection business and at first, I'm here just to protect your physical body. But being in close quarters with someone changes things after a while. And many of my clients feel comfortable opening up to me about other matters as well."

"Well, that's not going to be me," I say categorically.

"That's fine," he says, giving me permission to stay quiet as if I needed it.

I roll my eyes.

Martin is trying to be helpful and I know that I am misdirecting my anger by pointing at him, but unfortunately, he's the only one around. Jackson isn't here.

"Just so you know, I have a Master's degree in Psychology and Counseling. I'm a therapist, a professional listener. So, you can tell me anything you want at any time and I will be here for you."

"What do you mean?" I ask, taken a little aback by the news.

"Well, whatever you tell me, I will keep entirely to myself. So, you don't have to worry about anything getting back to Julie, or Jackson, or anyone. I take my oath as a therapist very seriously."

I sit back into the cushions of the couch and let them form a cocoon around me.

"So, why are you doing this?" I ask.

"It's a really good job. I got my counseling degree about a year ago and I've been a bodyguard for much longer than that. The main reason I even pursued it is because many of my clients would reach out to me and talk to me about their problems throughout the process and I wanted to figure out a better way to help them."

"What was the most important thing that you learned?"

"To listen," he says without missing a beat.

"What do you mean?"

"When my clients would talk to me before, I would try to immediately solve their problem. I would immediately make suggestions about what they should or shouldn't do to make things better in their life. But going through school, I realized that what makes someone a good therapist or a bad therapist is their ability to listen. I make suggestions sometimes, yes, but that's not the point. The point is to listen and ask questions that will lead my clients to make the best decisions for themselves. Because, the thing is that there is no right or wrong way to do things. It's all about what is right or wrong for you in this particular situation."

I bring my knees up to my chest and wrap my arms around them.

Martin leans back in the couch and just relaxes. If he is waiting for me to say something, he doesn't let on.

He doesn't make me feel uncomfortable about it. He doesn't push me to speak. Instead, we sit in a comfortable silence for a bit until my phone beeps. I look at the screen.

It's a call from Jackson.

I don't even bother to press the ignore button, instead I just let it ring until it stops. Then a text arrives.

HARLEY, please call me back. I really need to speak with you. I'm so sorry about everything.

IT'S FOLLOWED BY ANOTHER.

I HAVE A LOT TO EXPLAIN. Please let me talk to you. I love you.

"WHAT DO you think I should do?" I ask, handing him my phone. Martin gives me a smile.

"Is that a challenge?" he asks.

I guess it kind of came out that way, but it's not really. The truth is that I don't really know what to do.

"Why don't we start like this, instead?" he

says. "Why don't you tell me what you're thinking right now?"

I take a deep breath. That's a much harder place to start. I'd rather hear his answer, but I know that he's not going to give one.

29

HARLEY

WHEN WE TALK...

Martin asks me what I'm thinking right now and I try to focus all of the emotions that I'm feeling into words.

Blood pulses through my head, pounding hard in between my temples.

Tears tingle at the inside of my eyes and feel like they are only a breath away.

My chest seizes up, making it painful to take in air.

"Angry," I finally say. "I feel angry."

He nods. I want to say something else, but nothing else comes out.

"Good, keep going," he urges me.

"I don't know what else to say," I say, shaking my head.

"You said you feel angry. What are you angry about?"

"You know." I grit my teeth.

"I know the general circumstances, but not... the details."

"You want me to just lay them out for you?"

He nods.

I want to fight him. I want to say that I don't want to tell him a word, but that wouldn't be true.

In reality, I'm glad that he's pushing me to talk. I have been bottling this up enough as it is.

"I'm just...mad. Mad as hell."

He nods without saying a word. Just waits.

"Who does he think he is? I mean, how could he just break up with me like that? Without so much as an explanation? I deserve a lot better."

Somewhere from the corner of my eye I see him nodding again.

But his encouragement is no longer important.

The words are steam rolling out of me.

I open my mouth and every shitty thing that I have felt ever since he dumped me comes rolling out.

"The thing that I'm most mad about though is that I was such an idiot. I mean, I have always been very cautious about relationships. But when it came to Jackson...I let my guard down. And now, look at me! He left me and I'm pregnant and alone. I still have that stalker after me. I'm living in a studio apartment with a girl who is getting really sick of my shit and whose boyfriend is my bodyguard, and now I guess, technically my therapist."

"Let's go back, for just a moment," Martin says. "I saw the texts that Jackson sent. Why didn't you let him back in?"

"I don't want to hear it," I say categorically. "I'm not one of those women, you know. One of those women who men can just dump and walk away from then come back to. No, I'm not the forgiving kind."

"What about the pregnancy?"

"What about that?"

"Have you made a decision?"

I take a deep breath. I look up at him. Our eyes meet and I dart mine away. I don't dare hold his gaze for long.

"No, I haven't," I say slowly.

"Do you think that might have been one of

the reasons why you didn't want to let Jackson in here?"

I look down at my stomach. "It's not like it's very visible that I'm pregnant, right?"

"No, not at all." Martin smiles. "I am just thinking that it might have something to do with the guilt."

I look down at the floor.

He's right.

Of course, he's right.

I do feel guilty. I am guilty. I know that this is not a decision that I should be making alone.

Jackson is the father and he needs to know. But the pain that he has caused me...it's just too much to bear.

And what if he doesn't want me to keep it?

Or what if he does?

Both options send shivers down my arms.

The truth is that I don't know how I feel about this and I'm afraid that if I were to tell him then I will let his opinion of the situation sway me.

"I just need more time."

"More time for what?" Martin asks.

"I need more time to figure out what I should do."

He nods.

"I'm not ready to be a mother. I mean, I have no money. I live in a shoebox and I can barely afford that. If I were to have this baby then I'll have to move back in with my parents. There would be no other way."

"What about Jackson?"

"What about him?"

"Well, he is the father, right?"

"Right."

"And he is definitely a man of substantial means. I do not think that he would mind supporting you and his child in a comfortable way. Not at all."

"No, no, no," I say, shaking my head so feverishly that my neck starts to hurt.

"What's wrong with that?"

"I can't..." My words trail off. I don't know what I mean. I don't know what I'm saying.

"I can't do that," I say after taking a deep breath.

"What do you mean?"

"I can't tell him. Not until I decide what I want for myself."

"Are you thinking of not telling him at all?" Martin asks after a moment.

I focus my gaze on him. Narrowing my eyes, I ask, "You're not going to tell him about this conversation, right?"

"Of course not. I take my patient confidentiality very seriously."

I don't really believe him, but I don't really have a choice. "Even though he is paying you?"

"It doesn't matter who is paying me, Harley. I am your bodyguard and I am your therapist. My allegiance is to you and to your secrets."

My secret.

Is that what my baby is? A secret?

I guess so. Hmm...that's disheartening.

I never really gave having kids much thought but I never expected the news to be a secret.

A big lump forms in the back of my throat.

I don't want my baby to be a secret. I don't want my baby to think that he or she isn't loved every moment of every day. I take a deep breath and wipe the tear that runs down my cheek. Well, there it is, huh? I guess there's nothing else left to decide about this.

"What is it?" Martin asks. "You suddenly have this aura around you. Something is different."

I give him a weak smile.

"You caught that, huh?" I ask.

He raises his eyebrows and waits for me to answer.

"I was just thinking about the baby and how I never thought that my baby would be a secret. I always thought that this would be a happy time. And that's when I realized that I have already made the decision about what I'm going to do about this."

"What is that?"

"No matter how sick I am right now, or how unprepared I am to have a baby or how poor, I'm going to keep it."

30

HARLEY

WHEN I MAKE A DISCOVERY...

Making the decision to keep the baby takes a weight off my shoulders.

There's something about not knowing that puts you into a purgatory of anxiety.

And now that I've made the decision to keep it and to raise it myself, everything seems easier.

It's like the load that I am carrying up to the two-hundredth floor of a high-rise is suddenly half the weight it was before and I am twice as strong.

I get off the couch and make myself a cup of tea.

Martin joins me.

Cradling the warm cup in my hands, I watch the steam rise up in front of us.

It swirls off the surface of the water, slowly and whimsically making it toward my face.

I bring the cup closer to my eyes and close them, letting the steam caress my skin.

"I think that the scariest thing about having a child, for me, is the whole unknown aspect to it."

Martin nods.

"I just don't know what it will be like. I mean, there are women who are born with this innate feeling of knowing that they want a baby. And I just never felt that. Never. I mean, I always knew that I wanted to be a writer, but to have a baby? To create life? No, that was always for someone else."

"And now?"

"Nothing has really changed. I mean, if I weren't pregnant then I still wouldn't be dreaming of having a baby. But now that it's happening, I just sort of wonder...why not? What if it's...extraordinary?"

***

THE LONGER I talk to Martin, the easier the words come out. And the longer I talk to him, the more centered I get about what I want.

That's the thing about talking, or writing, isn't it?

Sometimes, you need to separate yourself from your thoughts and actually put them into words, either by saying them out loud or by writing them down.

And it's only then that all the stuff swirling around in my mind becomes focused and clear.

When Martin excuses himself to make a phone call, I pick up my laptop. I stare at the typed words which only have a paragraph into chapter twenty-nine as well as the notes as to what to write next in this chapter.

But suddenly, I'm not feeling it.

Not the subject matter, but the writing.

My thoughts drift and, instead I open the main Kindle Direct Publishing tab. I haven't been here in a few days.

Yesterday was the end of the month and it would be nice to tally up the total sales.

My heart pounds as the main page loads. What if the books that I sold is suddenly zero? I click on Reports, holding my breath.

Oh.

My.

God.

No, this can't be right. I stare at the screen. There are little bar graphs across each day of the month. I hover the mouse over each one to see how many sales I've had.

I quickly make a note of how many total units I sold on Amazon before clicking over to Apple, then to Barnes and Noble, Google Play, and Kobo.

From a book priced at $3.99, I make about 70% (there's an additional delivery fee as well from Amazon).

So, I take home about $2.70 from each book. This month I sold a total of 1,391 books for a total of $3,756 across all retailers!

I stare at that number in disbelief. Almost fourteen hundred people bought my books during these thirty days.

My eyes light up and a big smile grows on my face.

Of course, I also spent some money on Facebook advertising in order to generate those sales. I click over to the Ads Manager platform to see how much the total damage was.

I spent a total of $1256.

Wow.

That's a big number, of course.

But Jackson assured me that I needed to spend money on advertising in order to find readers. I mean, how else would anyone find out about me?

And given the results, that money really paid off. I spent $1250 and generated $3756 in total sales.

My profit for the month is $2,506 with a 66.72% return on investment.

Still unable to believe the numbers completely, I stare at the calculator on my phone and run through them again.

Is this right?

Did I really just make twenty-five hundred dollars in profit off my writing?

Another thousand and I will be more than able to cover all of my bills without getting a proper job.

More than that, I'll be able to pay Jackson back with the money that he had '*lent*' me.

It wasn't really a loan, it was more of a gift, or maybe a pay-off. But when I accepted it, I promised myself that I would pay back every last cent and now, I'm actually on my way to doing that.

My stomach growls and I place my hand over it.

"I'm actually going to be able to support you doing what I love," I whisper under my breath. "I'm going to be able to be home with you, watch you grow up, and do the one thing that I have wanted to do since I was a little girl."

31

JACKSON

WHEN I HAVE TO WORK...

B eing forced to work somewhere you do not want to work, to do something you don't want to do, is one of those mundane parts of life.

Many people have to work at places they hate just to make a living, just to pay the bills, just to keep the roof over their heads.

But I am not someone who is used to this.

I have always made my own way in life. I never worked jobs I hated. I survived on very little, a lot less than most, just to live according to my own rules.

And now? Now, sitting at my desk, talking to the heads of departments and pretending that I am still in charge, it feels a lot like torture.

I keep glancing at the clock and the hours go

by at a snail's pace. Every time I look at the time, only a few minutes have passed.

And it's just the second day.

No, I can't keep at it this way. Something has got to give.

I try to go through the motions. I try to think about what the best thing I can do for this company is, but Minetta no longer feels like it belongs to me at all.

It's like this foreign thing. Some place that I once worked, that once meant everything to me.

During a conference call, my mind wanders and I catch myself thinking about Harley.

This isn't unusual, of course. I think about her all the time, but even more so now. How can I keep working here?

How can I stay on as CEO when I hate everything about my current position? But watching my employees give their presentations on the video screen, I know that I can't just leave them.

If I were to step down now, then they would all be fired.

Andrew Lindell isn't someone to fuck around with and I refuse to leave them at the mercy of that asshole. No, I will stay here and fight.

He made promises, many of which he has
not kept. That's fine. That's the kind of person
that he is. But I am not. When I make promises,
then I do my best to keep them. I cannot let these
people lose their jobs. I will do everything in my
power to stop it. But how?

I don't know the answer to that any more
than I know how to get Harley back. The
reasons for pushing her away seem as stupid
and ill-advised as the ones I once made with
the Lindells. That's the thing about being
foolish; you never really know when you're
doing the wrong thing until you have already
done it.

I can't turn back time, but I can do my best to
remedy this situation now. I thank everyone for
their time and say my goodbyes.

I do all of this in a daze.

I can keep this up, but it won't do anyone any
good. I need a plan to take back my company. But
first, I need a plan to get back my girlfriend and
make her my wife.

I CHANGE into my sweats and run down the stairs

and out of the front door. I haven't gone on a run in a long time, and at first my lungs burn.

I keep running, not at a very fast pace, but at one that's good enough, and my body quickly adapts.

The labored breaths disappear after a while, taking with them the pounding headache that has dominated my mind for most of the day.

I run past old women pushing strollers full of groceries and young moms holding their toddler's hands as they cross the street.

I run past a corgi in a knitted vest and booties and a greyhound leading his owner by the leash.

I run past a doorman who nods his head slightly in my direction and a homeless man who doesn't even look up at me.

I run past numerous cars waiting for the light to turn green as well as a few motorcycles and couriers on bicycles.

I'm not going anywhere in particular, at least that's what I think at first. But then I discover that actually I am.

My legs are taking me somewhere very specific and it's only when I'm a few streets away from her house that I realize where I am.

I am going to see Harley.

Or at least, I'm going to see her call box.

The closer I get, the more I realize that it is quite unlikely that she will let me in again or give me any sort of time to explain myself.

So, what can I do?

How can I make her understand?

How can I make her give me a chance to even say a word?

Then other thoughts start to creep in.

Maybe I should put this to the side.

Maybe I should respect her position and not try to force her to talk to me. I mean, isn't that a sign of respect? She wants space and I should give it to her, right?

Parker didn't think so. He wanted to make sure that she listened to him. He fought for the right to speak to her and he just made things worse. I can't follow in his footsteps.

But when I see her building and look up at the window that I know belongs to her, I can't force myself away. It's like there's some sort of magnetic force pulling me closer to her.

I don't want to be a stalker. I don't want to disrespect her position. I don't want to frighten her. I don't want to push myself on her. But I have to take another chance. I am not Parker. I am just a man who made a terrible mistake. I love her and there was a time when she loved me and then I fucked it all up. Now, I just need to make it right.

I am tempted to go up to the call box and press the button of her apartment again, but something stops me.

She will see my face, and she won't let me inside. If she doesn't then Martin or Julie will and they won't let me up.

So, what then?

No, if I want to see her then I need an element of surprise.

And that's when the opportunity suddenly presents itself. The front door opens and Martin and Julie walk out. He takes her hand to cross the street and they disappear around the corner.

32

JACKSON

WHEN I MAKE MY WAY INSIDE...

The irony of the situation isn't lost on me. I hired Harley protection services that I now have to evade in order to talk to her.

I watch the corner to make sure that Martin doesn't come back at the same time as I'm watching the front door to her building. I need a way in.

I can either press the number of one of her neighbors and make up some story to get in, or wait for someone to come out. Before I can make a decision one way or another, an older woman pulling a cart behind her comes to the door.

"Here, let me help you with that." I quickly jump to her aid, nearly knocking her over in all of my excitement. Stay calm. Don't make her suspicious. Just breathe.

"Thank you very much, young man," the woman says in the coarse voice of a lifelong smoker.

"You're very welcome," I say, holding the door behind her. I wait for her to get a little bit further away from me so I can slip in without notice.

"Aren't you going to close that?" she asks, turning around at the last second.

"Um...actually, I'm going up to see a friend of mine."

"Oh, yeah? What apartment?"

My mind goes blank. The only number I can think of is the one that belongs to Harley, so that's the one I say.

"I don't know how those two girls live in that small space," she says, shaking her head. "But then again, I wasn't the one who got along well with other girls, if you know what I mean."

She laughs at her own joke and I laugh along with her, even though I don't quite know what she's getting at.

"I used to be a dancer. Back in the 60s. I danced at all of the big clubs in mid-town.

People came all the way from Vermont and Montauk to see me."

"That must've been great," I say, still holding onto the door, hoping that she will let me go before Martin and Julie come back and find me here.

"I didn't always look like this, sonny. There was a time when I had all the curves and all the moves to make men go wild."

I have to change my approach. Maybe flattering her will move this whole thing along faster.

"Oh, c'mon now," I say in my most relaxed voice. "You are quite a looker. I bet you still bring men to their knees."

She throws her head back in laughter. For a moment there I can see her as she was all those years ago. Young, beautiful, and full of life.

"You are a keeper!" she says, waving her finger in my direction and heading down the street with a newfound pep in her step.

"It was great talking to you! I yell after her.

Right before I disappear into the lobby, I hear her say, "If one of those girls doesn't want you, you come knock on apartment #417!"

WHEN I GET to Harley's apartment, the smile that her neighbor put on my face vanishes.

My heart jumps into my throat.

What the hell do I do now that I'm here?

I run my fingertips over the grain in the wood and try to gather my thoughts.

I should just knock. I make a fist and lift it up into the air. But something stops me.

Fear? Of course.

There are only so many times that you can ask someone to talk to you and hear no. There are only so many chances and after that?

I have to respect her position. If I keep trying to get her to listen to me against her will, well, at that point I'm no better than Parker. I get it now. That feeling of desperation that he must've felt.

The first few times he made contact, they had friendly exchanges. He was led to believe that she might actually be interested.

No, I'm not foolish enough to blame her.

She was just being nice and polite, the way that women often are when they are put into an uncomfortable situation that they don't know how to extricate themselves from.

The last thing that I want to do is to become a stalker.

The last thing I want to do is to scare her or cross any boundaries. I love her and I want her to be happy.

But I also want her to be happy with me. I want her to give me another chance even though I don't think I deserve it.

I should just knock.

She's home.

She will answer.

And then...then I will finally see her face. Then she will finally see mine and things will be different than they are through the camera downstairs. I make a fist again. I bring it to the door.

But then I pull away just before making contact. The thing is that she had already seen my face. I am sure of it.

She saw me pleading for her to open the door and she didn't.

What if that means that she never wants to speak to me again?

Does this mean that I have to accept that we are over...for good?

I take a step away from the door and turn around.

My shoulders hang down as reality starts to set in. Perhaps, this is it for us. I've done my best and she still doesn't want me.

What else is there to do?

My eyes drop down to the floor. The wood is old and scuffed up, torn up by years of shuffled feet. How many other people have stood right here in this same spot fighting their own demons just like I am fighting mine?

"Here, let me help you."

His voice stops me in my tracks. It belongs to Martin and it's coming from around the corner. Shit. What do I do now?

33

JACKSON

WHEN IT'S ALMOST ALL OVER...

Martin is with someone. I can hear their muffled voices along with his. Something is holding them all back, giving me a moment to think.

But time is running out. I glance over my shoulder at the window at the end of the hallway.

It's as old as the rest of the building with thick elaborate molding framing the ancient glass.

To open it, you have to pull it up by the little hooks at either side of the ledge, but no matter how hard I pull, it doesn't open.

Years of gunk and grime has permanently

sealed this relic and I stare at the fire escape on the other side, wistfully.

I take a deep breath.

They are going to come around the corner any moment now and see me. There's nowhere to go now, so I stand right next to Harley's door and brace myself for impact.

I wait.

Then I wait some more.

For a second, I'm almost tempted to go out there and see what's taking them so long.

But instead, I run my hand down the frame of the door and over the handle. When I try it, much to my surprise, it turns.

"Thank you again for helping." I hear a female voice say as I slip inside.

Despite the age and the disrepair of this building, the door surprisingly doesn't creak and I'm able to close it without making a sound.

From the foyer, I see her. Her hair is piled on the top of her head and tied up in a loose messy bun.

She is sitting at her desk, facing the screen of her laptop.

Before slipping through the open bathroom

door into the only other room in the apartment, I watch her.

She types fast while bobbing her head slightly from side to side while listening to music on her wireless earphones.

It takes all of my energy not to call out her name and take her into my arms right there. But that would be the worst thing I could do right now. When I hear the keys going into the doorknob, I close the bathroom door behind me and wait.

"Harley, the front door was open," Martin says, coming in.

She doesn't respond. He calls her name again and she shrieks. The sound is loud and high-pitched. It sounds exactly like the one I heard outside of my door the first night we met. I ball up my fists and fight the urge to go out and help her.

"Oh my God, you scared me!" I hear her say.

"I distinctly remember locking the door," Martin lectures.

"Yeah, Mrs. Crawford stopped by for a second and I guess I must've forgotten to lock it after I talked to her."

"You really have to be more careful," Martin

insists. I hate the way he speaks to her. As if she is ten years old and he is her father. But he's just doing his job. And he's very good at it. Except for the fact that he did leave her unattended today, which he wasn't supposed to do without getting another person to fill in.

"Detective Richardson," Harley says. "I didn't see you there."

A gulp forms in the back of my throat. What is she doing here?

The walls of the bathroom aren't very thin and I can't make out the majority of what is being said. While I try, my thoughts start to swirl around my head.

I should not be here.

It's one thing to ring her doorbell. It's another to knock on her apartment door. But this?

Hiding out in her bathroom?

How can I possibly explain this?

Regret grabs ahold of me and wraps its cold hands around my throat, tightening its grip.

They are going to find me here. I'm trespassing on private property stalking a victim of a kidnapping.

And if Detective Richardson finds me here?

I look around the room. To say that it's

cramped would be the understatement of a lifetime.

There's barely any room to get around at all. And more importantly, there's nowhere to go.

It doesn't have a window so the only way out of this mess is the exact way that I got in.

And I can't risk trying to go out the front door with so many people standing only a few feet away.

Harley starts to cry. I hear her thick sobs clearly through the wall of the shower. I close the curtain slowly in front of me, giving myself a fathom of privacy, just in case someone decides to use the toilet.

"I'm really sorry about the bad news." I hear Detective Richardson say.

"How can they just let him out?" another female voice asks. It must belong to Julie.

"Didn't they catch him with all of that crystal meth? Shouldn't he do time for that?"

"Sam has contact with the FBI and the police. He is a well-connected informant. Of course, I don't have direct proof of this, but that's what my sources tell me."

"So, what does that mean?" Harley asks.

"It means that he is a very valuable asset to a

number of investigators and that means that they need him out on the streets doing his thing in order to close cases."

"But what about what he did to me?"

I can't see her, but I can almost feel her shrug her shoulders.

She is probably even tilting her head to the side right about now, trying to make it seem like none of this is her fault.

I know the truth.

She's incompetent. Her whole department is useless. If they weren't then both men who kidnapped Harley would be behind bars where they deserve to be. Or better yet, dead.

"What do I do now?" Harley asks.

34

JACKSON

WHEN IT'S ONLY THE BEGINNING...

"Just stay put like you are doing now. Stay inside. Stay safe," Detective Richardson suggests.

There's a moment of silence. I press my ear closer to the subway tiles to see if I'm missing anything.

Then she starts to laugh. The sound is quiet at first but builds quickly into something seesawing between joy and mockery.

"So, let me get this straight?" Harley asks. "You don't know where Parker Huntington is, the man who kidnapped me and kept me tied up in a cabin in the North woods. And the other kidnapper? You just let him go, right?"

No one responds.

"And as for me? You think that *my* best plan of action is to stay put?"

I can almost hear the sarcasm in her voice.

"So, basically, I'm the one who will be serving time in prison, right? I'm the one who has to live my life in seclusion. Only go outside with a bodyguard? Everyone else, the people who did this to me, they can just go on with their lives as if they did nothing wrong."

Again, no one says anything.

I reach for the shower curtain to run out there and take her into my arms, but I stop myself.

Why are they being quiet? Don't they see how much she's suffering? Don't they want to help her?

"I'm fine, Julie. I'm fine." I hear her say and I let out a deep breath that I've been holding in.

I wonder if this is my chance to escape without being seen. If they are all standing away from the front door, facing the windows out front, then I can slip out just like I had slipped in.

But I have no guarantee of where they are standing.

Besides, Martin is quite good at his job. He may have made a bad decision in leaving her alone but is quick on his feet and aware of his surroundings. No, I should stay in this shower until they all clear out. Or at least, Detective Richardson does.

I hear someone heading toward the door. Is she finally leaving?

I hear a door swing open.

For a moment, I think it's the front door, but the light that streams into this room confirms my worst suspicion. Now, there's only a thin vinyl curtain separating me and the person on the other side.

I hold my breath and tuck myself closer against the wall.

This room isn't well heated, and the chill bites at my skin.

In my effort to disappear, it dawns on me that I had closed my eyes. I open them slightly to a small slit and focus. Through the happy orange fish smiling at each other, I see that it's her.

Harley turns on the faucet and bends at the waist. She scoops water into her palms and throws it on her face. With her eyes still shut, she feels around for a towel above the toilet. When she finds it, she buries her head in it.

I want to reach for her. I want to take her into

my arms and tell her that it's all going to be okay. When I peel myself off the wall, my knee cracks and she pauses. I freeze and wait.

Neither of us makes a move for a moment and I pray that she doesn't pay much attention to the sound that she has just heard.

How many times do we hear something that sounds like something else?

All the time. Please, let this be one of those times.

Paused in suspended animation, I wait.

And wait.

She hangs the towel back on the door and looks at herself in the mirror.

I can see my own reflection in it, but it's grainy and only one of those things that you would notice if you knew what you were looking for; a man hiding in your shower stall.

I allow myself to exhale but only for a moment. To not upset the equilibrium of the room, I take in a breath just as quickly.

She turns the handle of the door and I finally look away from her. It's almost over. Just wait a few more moments and everything will be okay.

"What are you doing here?" Harley hisses,

pulling the shower curtain back and exposing me for the creep that I am.

My heart jumps into my throat as I stare at her unable to speak.

"What are you doing here, Jackson?" she asks again. The tone of her voice is disapproving and discontent. But quiet. She doesn't raise her voice, probably because she doesn't want anyone out there to know what's going on in here.

"You have ten seconds to tell me before I scream," she threatens.

35

JACKSON

WHEN THEY FIND ME...

I have practiced what I would say were she to give me another chance numerous times before.

I have practiced both long and short speeches, but I never practiced what I would say after she caught me hiding in her bathroom.

My mind goes blank and whatever I was going to say I forget completely. Instead, I just open my mouth and start talking.

"I love you. I have always loved you. The only reason I broke up with you was to protect you. I had bad people after me and I thought that if they didn't know that you existed then everything would be okay. But as it often is in life, things don't work out like we plan."

"You really hurt me," she says.

Her eyes narrow as she gives me a look of total pain.

I know that there isn't much I can say at this moment to make things right, but I have to try.

This is the only opportunity I might ever have.

"The reason I've been calling you and texting you and coming here...the reason I snuck in here while Martin was gone was that I needed to tell you that...I want you back. I love you and I want to be with you...forever."

The corners of her lips curl up for a moment forming the beginning of a smile. But a second later, that embryo of a smile vanishes as quickly as it shows up.

"I can't do this," Harley says quietly.

"Do what?"

"I can't be one of those couples that keeps breaking up and getting back together all the time."

"I don't want that either."

I climb out of the shower and take a step closer to her. I put my hands on her shoulders. She tilts her head in the air and stares at me.

"Harley, please. Let's just...talk about this."

The way she is looking at me, the moment feels right. I move an inch closer to her and I press my lips onto hers.

"Get the hell away from me," she hisses, pushing me away.

Before I can even really process what just happened, the door behind me swings open hitting me in the back.

"Get down!" Martin screams into my ear. I drop to my knees as soon as he presses the barrel of the gun to the back of my head.

"No, no, no, it's fine! I'm fine," Harley mumbles.

Her words come out slurred in all the excitement.

The round metal feels cold and hard against the nape of my neck and I hold my breath, hoping that a bullet doesn't come out of there by accident.

"Please, please, put that away!" Harley pleads, getting in between us and now it's my turn to protect her. It's one thing for him to point the gun at me. But it's entirely another thing for him to point it at her. That, I cannot allow.

"Martin, it's me. I'm not here to hurt her."

I turn to face him, holding Harley out of the way of the prospective bullet. Finally, he drops his hand down to his side.

Harley collapses into my arms with tears streaming down her face. Her whole body is shaking.

"I think I'm going to be sick," she mumbles.

It feels like an hour has passed since Harley first caught me in her shower, but it has only been a matter of seconds.

Martin says something to me, along with Detective Richardson and Julie who are hovering somewhere in the foyer, not far away from us, but I'm entirely focused on Harley.

This whole thing brings her to her knees and she pushes both me and Martin out of the way to get to the floor.

"What's wrong? Are you okay?" I ask, getting down next to her and pulling her hair out of the way.

She buries her head in the toilet and throws up. While I hold her, a wave of guilt comes over me.

How could I scare her so much?

How could I think that this was a good idea?

I knew that Martin was there. Of course, he would pull out his gun. It's his job, that's why I hired him.

Out of the corner of my eye, I glance over at Martin.

He disappears into the main room along with Detective Richardson. Only Julie keeps hanging around the doorway asking Harley if there's something she can do.

"No, I'm fine," Harley finally mumbles, wiping her mouth and flushing the toilet. Her whole body is drenched in sweat and her skin turns the color of porcelain. I help her to her feet.

"I'm so sorry that I scared you so much," I say over and over again as she washes her face in the sink and brushes her teeth.

"I should've never hidden here. I should have never scared you like this."

After putting the brush back in its holder she wipes her hands on the towel and turns to face me.

"You shouldn't have snuck in here. You shouldn't have scared me. But that's not why I got sick."

"What do you mean?" I ask, as a myriad of

reasons for what could've made her throw up run through my mind. My thoughts immediately go to the most tragic. Is she really ill? Does she have cancer? Is she dying?

"Jackson, I'm pregnant."

36

HARLEY

WHEN IT'S HIM...

I can't believe it's him. He is actually standing before me and asking me to take him back.

I have dreamed of this moment. I had imagined it a hundred times, but never did I think it would happen like this.

Of course, I got scared when I first felt the presence of a strange man in my bathroom.

I froze.

It's as if my whole body has gone into shock.

It has to be Parker.

I just know it.

He finally found me and this will be the end.

But then the figure moves just slightly out of the way of the tangerine-colored fish.

His hair falls out of his face just for a second. That's enough for me to recognize him.

Jackson Ludlow.

He forced himself in despite my best efforts to keep him out.

What is it that they say about romantic heroes?

In movies and books, they always act like stalkers.

Well, I have a real stalker. And the truth is that they don't.

There's a difference between someone who pushes past all of your boundaries to hurt you and someone who does it to get to you.

They are merely shades of the same thing but those distinctions make all the difference.

When I see him, I'm not afraid. I'm angry. A part of me is disappointed even. Not in him being here, but in the fact that it took so long for him to come.

Why did you wait? Why did you leave me alone for so long? Why did you listen when I pushed you away?

He tells me why he broke my heart, but none of those things make any sense. Someone is after him?

What does that have to do with me?

Why hurt the one person who was there for you?

The one person who stood by you and brought you out into the light.

Were it not for me, you'd still be wandering the hallways of your mansion all alone. And now? Now, everything is fucked.

Jackson takes a step closer to me.

He waits for me to respond. I don't, so he takes that as a sign to go ahead.

He presses his lips onto mine, and that's when I have had enough. Who do you think you are? You break my heart. You apologize. I don't accept your apology, but you just go ahead and try to kiss me anyway.

"Get the hell away from me," I whisper under my breath and push him away. He doesn't have the right to do this. He doesn't have the right to be here. No matter how much I wanted him to come. No matter how much I prayed for this very thing, now that he's here, I don't want to see him.

My thoughts go in circles over everything that has happened. The one thing I don't think about is Martin. I forget about the bodyguard who is currently speaking to a detective in the main room about my previous stalking situation. No, I don't give them any thought.

Not until he has his gun pointed at Jackson and my whole world flashes before my eyes.

Time stands still and I feel like I'm about to lose him. I'm watching the worst day in my life in slow motion.

If Martin were to shoot right now, the one person who means everything to me would disappear. The only thing I would have left is this feeling of overwhelming regret.

I force myself in between them.

I beg Martin to put the gun down.

Jackson fights me on this. He had cooperated by getting down on his knees only a moment before, but when I start to protest, he comes to my side, making everything worse.

But I know the truth. It's not him who made things worse. It was me. I have to stop this. I have to make him calm down.

I glance into Martin's eyes. There's nothing erratic in them. They are focused. Determined. If he were to shoot Jackson right now, it would be on purpose. But there's nothing I can do.

I try to get past Jackson to get in between

Martin and him, but he stops me. He blocks me with his body.

I hold my breath and wait. Finally, after what feels like a century, Martin drops the gun.

And that's when the wave of nausea hits me with hurricane gale speed. I don't have time to think. I push past both of them and barely have enough time to open the lid before it all comes spilling out.

Jackson leaps toward me, apologizing and asking me questions that I cannot physically answer. But he does hold my hair out of the way, and that is everything.

Afterward, I tell him the truth.

Why?

What would be the point of lying? I've made up my mind about what I'm going to do. Julie and Martin already know. He's the father. He should know as well.

"Jackson, I'm pregnant," I say.

37

HARLEY

This sentence isn't planned, so the words come out cold and unaffected. But that's not how I feel at all.

I feel everything but that, but I hide that away within me for protection. If you're not careful with your feelings, people might find out the truth.

And then what?

What if I were to tell him that I love him?

What if I were to tell him that he is the only person I want to have this baby with? That he makes me feel like everything is going to be okay, even though right now, it seems like it's the one thing that can't possibly happen.

"You're...pregnant?" Jackson asks.

He tilts his head as he looks at me perplexed.

He doesn't seem angry.

He doesn't seem disappointed.

He doesn't seem...anything. This lack of a reaction is what I'm not ready for.

"But how? We used...protection."

I shrug and look away. His question makes it sound like it's my fault when he was the one who bought it and put it on.

"I'm sorry, I shouldn't have said that. I'm just...surprised."

I shrug and hang my head.

I know that he has to have time to process this. I know that it had taken me a while before I was genuinely happy with the news, but that doesn't stop me from wanting to see him smile at this moment.

"What are you going to do?" Jackson asks. I lick my lips and take a step away from him. He takes a deep breath, as if he is bracing for impact.

"I would like to keep it," I say quietly.

I feel guilty that this decision is entirely up to me and I quickly add, "You don't have to do anything. You don't have to be involved if you don't want to be. I just wanted to tell you. I thought that you should know."

"You don't want me to be involved?" he asks, looking crestfallen.

"No...that's not what I said. I just don't want you to feel pressured to...do anything."

"You are having my child. Of course I will feel pressure, but that's a good thing. I want to be there. For you. For our baby."

Our baby. His words echo in my mind and I like the way they sound.

I nod. He kneels down before me and takes my hand in his.

"Harley, I am so, so sorry about everything."

His hand cradles mine and he brings it to his lips as he speaks.

"Please come back to me. Please give me another chance. I love you. More than anything in the world."

I want to tell him that I love him, too, but something is holding me back. I open my mouth, but I can't physically say the words.

Perhaps, it's too soon.

Maybe it's because I need more of an explanation.

I pull Jackson up to his feet and wrap my arms around him. We stand there in our embrace for a few moments before I pull away.

"C'mon, let's get out of this bathroom," I say.

He follows me back into the main room.

Detective Richardson, Julie, and Martin all have the same expression on their face.

They have been spying on us this whole time, but now they are pretending that they were talking about something else altogether.

"Well, I best be going," Detective Richardson says and no one stops her.

I thank her for her update, even though I think she could've just as easily used a phone or better yet, a text message.

The kind of news she delivered wasn't exactly uplifting and sometimes bad news is a lot easier to stomach at a distance.

After she leaves, Martin and Julie don't hang around much longer.

Martin pulls me aside and asks me if I'm comfortable staying alone with Jackson and then takes Julie by the arm and escorts her to dinner.

For once, I'm glad that our apartment is so small that it forces people to leave it in order to give us privacy. I doubt we could've cleared everyone out so quickly from Jackson's mansion.

"We're alone now," Jackson says. "Finally."

I nod and shrug my shoulders all the way up to my ears.

"You're not going to tell me what you're thinking, are you?" he asks after a moment.

"The thing is that I don't really know what I'm thinking."

"What do you mean?"

"It's all very...complicated."

"This whole time I just wanted you to give me a chance to explain. That's why I broke into your house. That's why I hid in there. For a chance to set things right."

I furrow my brow.

I believe him, but his reasoning doesn't really make any sense.

Jackson paces back and forth.

I watch him walk from one side of the apartment to another.

Suddenly, he stops.

"Can I tell you a story?" he asks. I nod.

"A long time ago, I met a man named Andrew Lindell."

That's how Jackson dives into the past. He tells me about growing up with his parents, about the gambling debts, about trying to find money to grow his business.

He tells me about everything that he never told me about before and I listen. The more he talks, the more I learn about this man who I thought I knew.

Now, it looks like what I used to know about has barely scratched the surface of everything he was.

At the end, his voice gets quieter, and becomes barely audible. I lean closer to him, certain that I must not have heard him correctly.

"You own how much of Minetta now?"

"Nineteen percent," he repeats himself.

I shake my head.

"Why did you sign so much of it over?"

"I had no choice."

"So, what now?" I ask.

"Now, they are forcing me to stay on or they will fire everyone there. Now, I have to figure out some way to get rid of Lindell. Once and for all."

38

JACKSON

WHEN I TELL HER EVERYTHING...

To make amends for every mistake and bad call, I sit on the couch next to Harley and answer all of her questions.

I tell her about anything and everything and don't hesitate for a moment.

I have nothing to hide.

She listens.

Nods.

And then keeps asking the same question over and over again.

"But why? Why couldn't you just take me aside and tell me what was going on?"

I explain it over and over. The more I talk, the less I believe myself.

"It had to be a surprise, Harley. I couldn't tell

you what was really going on. I couldn't go into any of that. If they had questioned you, then they would've known immediately."

"You don't give me enough credit."

"You don't know these people."

"You don't think I could've kept your secret?"

"That's not what I meant and you know that," I insist.

She shakes her head.

"I wouldn't have told them about you."

"They wouldn't have asked nicely."

We go in circles without resolving one thing.

But this conversation is not really about a resolution.

It's about reaching an understanding.

She has to understand what I was dealing with and I have to understand how much I had hurt her.

"Looking back? What do you think?" she asks. "Was it a mistake?"

I shrug and look down at the floor. "I didn't know what they knew. All I wanted was for them to never know they had this bargaining chip."

"What do you mean?"

"You. If they knew that I cared about you then they would've taken you. They would've used you. They did anyway. So, it all sort of blew up in my face. But back then, I had no idea what would happen."

We sit in silence for a while, just looking at each other.

I try to read her face, but she keeps her expression stoic and tucked neatly away in a box that's deep below the surface.

My thoughts drift away from us and to the news that she had just shared. My lips form into a smile.

"What?" she asks. "Why are you smiling?"

"Just thinking about the baby."

"And?"

"And...I'm really excited. It's amazing."

She straightens her back. Her eyes dart to mine.

"You are?" Her lips soften and part.

I pull myself closer to her on the couch. I take her hands in mine. They fold into my palms to make a perfect fit.

I rub my thumbs over hers, lingering over the smoothness of her dark red nails.

"I never thought that I would want to have another child," I say slowly. "If you had brought up the idea of it, I would've probably said no, I don't want any more children. But when you told me that you were pregnant, everything was different."

"What do you mean?"

"It was no longer this possibility of what might happen in the future. It was what was already happening. And this reality made me happy."

She narrows her eyes, as if she doesn't quite believe me.

"I don't think I'm saying it right," I backtrack. I take a moment to collect my thoughts.

"What surprised me was how I felt in the moment when you told me that you were pregnant. My heart just filled with joy. And that was the most unexpected thing."

Finally, she smiles.

Her lips part slightly and her eyes twinkle. After giving me a little nod, she drops her head on my shoulder.

"When I first found out, I was really scared."

"Yeah, I can imagine."

"We weren't together and I wasn't sure if I was ever going to see you again. I didn't really want to."

"Of course not."

"Just the prospect of raising this baby on my own...I didn't think I could do it. And even if I could I didn't really want to."

"I understand."

We don't say anything for a while. I just hold her and wait.

"I hate to admit it, but the only thing I was thinking about at that time was me. I just felt so sorry for myself. I thought that being a mother would mean the end of everything. The end of all of my dreams, all of my goals. People say that you can have it all, but I couldn't imagine myself having it all. I mean, how could I have time to write if I had a baby?"

"You must have been terrified."

"Plus, on top of all that, I was really sick. And that was messing with my head big time. It's hard to think clearly and make a decision one way or another when you are sick to your stomach all day and all night long. I was sleep deprived and nauseated and I couldn't even make it to the next day let alone imagine what it would be like to have this baby on my own and deal with a child for years to come."

"I'm so sorry you were alone through all of this," I whisper, kissing the top of her head.

"But I got some medication which made things better. I'm still tired all the time and I feel nauseous every morning and I have very little energy but it's...manageable now."

"Harley, whatever you need from me, I am here for you."

She nods and leans into me more.

"I mean it." I tilt her head upward. "I am not sure where we stand as a couple, but I am here for you. I want to help you during this pregnancy. If you want, I'd love for you to move into my house. If you don't, then I can be here for you anytime you want. I can stay here or rent an apartment next door."

"What do you mean?"

"Just that. If you don't want me to stay here with you and you don't want to move into my house, I can rent a place next to you so I can help you with whatever you may need."

"But people live there now?"

"I'm sure that they can be convinced to leave for the right price."

She starts to laugh.

"What? What's so funny?"

"For a second there, I forgot that you were rich," she says, smiling.

"What do you mean?" I ask, also starting to laugh.

"Well, only a rich person would even think of *that* as being an option."

"What?"

"Going over to my neighbor's door, asking them to move out for nine months in exchange for a check."

I shrug. "What can I say? It's my experience that everything has a price. It just depends on how much you're willing to pay."

39

HARLEY

IN THE BEGINNING...

The next week is a blur.

I want to take things slowly, so we start to spend time together and get to know each other again.

Julie laughs every time Jackson comes over just to hang out, but it's what feels right for now.

It's not that I don't want him back.

I do.

More than anything.

But I also need time to heal.

What he did really hurt me, and while I now finally understand why, my understanding of the situation is still very cerebral.

I get it in my mind, but I don't get it in my heart.

The pain that I felt when he broke up with me is still there somehow, right below the surface.

And though I want more than anything to just jump into Jackson's arms again and live the rest of my life as if it never happened, there is a part of me that keeps wondering what if it happens again?

Even though Julie doesn't really understand this, Jackson does.

I think he thinks of himself as lucky that I'm even giving him another chance.

"I still don't see what the big deal is about me and Jackson going out alone," I say to Martin.

The three of us are hanging out in our kitchen, waiting for Jackson to come over. Up until this point, Jackson and I have just spent time here together. We haven't gone anywhere, not even his house.

But I am getting a bit sick of being cooped up in this studio all the time and am looking forward to a nice dinner out.

Alone.

"It's not safe," Martin says.

"You had no problem leaving us alone here."

"Yes, that's because I've secured this

apartment. No one can get up the fire escape. And there's another security detail posted at the front door while I'm gone."

"Nothing is going to happen. Jackson will be with me."

"Jackson isn't a trained bodyguard, Harley," Martin insists. I get the feeling that Jackson sneaking into this apartment without him knowing has hurt his ego and now he's being extra cautious about everything.

"I just left the door open before. It was nothing that you did."

"I should've had someone at that door so that he couldn't sneak in," he mumbles under his breath.

"See, it is all about you! You're just upset that someone got past you. Well, it's all fine. If he didn't then we probably wouldn't be together now."

"No." Martin shakes his head. "It's all about you. What if it weren't Jackson? What if it were Sam or Parker again? Or some nut job on Parker's behalf?"

I shrug.

"Things wouldn't have ended so nicely."

"Martin, calm down, you're getting all

worked up." Julie jumps to my defense. She puts her hand on his shoulder and rubs it a little.

But Martin isn't worked up at all.

He is calm and collected.

Composed.

"This isn't going to happen, Harley. Not as long as I am in your employ."

This takes me aback.

"What do you mean?"

"If you want to go out with Jackson on your own, then you have to fire me. Otherwise, I wouldn't be doing my job if I let you do this."

"Let's not get so serious," Julie says, rubbing his shoulder again. He shrugs her off.

"I am talking to my client, Julie. Can you give us some space?"

I take a deep breath.

"You don't have to blow this out of proportion," I say. He stares at me and waits.

AT DINNER, I yearn to order the most expensive cocktail on the menu, but I'm forced to drown my discontent in a non-alcoholic drink that doesn't even come close to taking the edge off.

Martin and Julie are sitting across from us, laughing and enjoying their beers. Jackson doesn't order a drink in solidarity with me even though I tell him that it's not necessary.

Still, I appreciate the gesture.

"Are you okay?" Julie whispers from across the booth.

Martin eyes me without saying a word.

"Look, it's not that I'm mad at you, Martin," I say, deciding to bring it out all into the open. "It's just that I'm annoyed. Pissed really."

"Why?" Julie asks.

"Just about everything. Sam and Parker are both out there living their lives as if they didn't do anything wrong. And I'm the one who feels like I'm in a fucking prison cell. I can't do anything. I can't go out alone. I can't go out on a date with the father of my baby. I can't have a drink. It's all...too much."

"I'm sorry," they all say. Jackson squeezes my hand under the table. I don't expect it to, but it does make me feel a little better.

"What would make me feel a lot better about you going outside by yourself," Martin says, "is if you weren't in the city. Maybe we can all go somewhere? A house in the country? With land

and a perimeter that can be secured safely. That way you won't see anyone watching you, but you'll feel safe."

That does sound nice. I look over at Julie. She has a big smile on her face. I glance at Jackson, who gives me a nod.

"That sounds wonderful," I say.

"Great, let's try to arrange something like that asap."

40

HARLEY

A FRESH START...

After we all share a slice of tiramisu, Julie and I excuse ourselves and go to the bathroom, leaving the boys to take care of the bill.

"Do you ever feel bad about Martin always paying the bill?" I ask, applying a fresh coat of lipstick in the mirror.

"No." She laughs. "I stopped asking a while ago."

She looks at herself in the mirror, fixing her messy bun by arranging each strand just so.

"You haven't even known each other *a while*," I point out, smiling.

"Really? It feels like we've known each other forever."

"That's 'cause you're sharing a postage stamp of an apartment with him."

"Okay, seriously, now. What do you think about him?"

"Who?"

"C'mon, don't play dumb. Martin."

I shrug.

"I don't think you should be asking my opinion on that."

"Why?" Julie looks at me surprised.

"Well, he's my *security detail*," I say, using his words. "So, I find him rather...annoying."

"Yes, I can see how annoying it would be to have someone around who cares whether you live or die."

I roll my eyes.

"He's good at his job," I finally say. "But it gets a bit too much. As you know. I mean, he's there all the time."

"You can always go to Jackson's."

"Then he'll be at Jackson's all the time."

"A twelve thousand square foot mansion is not the same thing as a studio apartment."

I shrug. "I do like his idea of getting out of the city for a bit. Might be nice to be able to go on a walk again," I say.

Julie nods, twirling the ends of her hair around her finger. She bites her lower lip. Then it hits me. She's nervous. I've been so self-involved this whole time that I hadn't even realized that she's asking something specific.

"What's wrong?"

"Nothing." She shrugs.

"C'mon, tell me. Why are you suddenly so interested in what I think about Martin? Since when did you ever need my approval of who to date?"

She bites her lower lip again and smiles with her eyes.

"'Cause he told me that he loves me. And I love him."

"Oh my God!" I squeal and grab her by the shoulders. "Really?"

"Really." She nods. "And he asked me to move in with him."

"Isn't he already living with you?" I joke.

"Ha, ha," she says, rolling her eyes.

I wrap my arms around her and whisper into her ear, "I'm so excited for you."

"I guess you are," she says, pulling away from me. "This was not the reaction that I was expecting."

"What do you mean?"

"Well, when I told you about Logan—"

"Logan is an asshole," I interrupt her.

"I know. But we didn't know that back then."

"Julie, when it comes to men you date, think of me like a dog. I can always smell the bad ones."

Her eyes twinkle, and she wipes a small tear out of the corner of the left one.

"What's wrong?" I pull her in closer to me.

"Nothing. I'm just so…happy. I really love him. We just mesh so well together," she says, intertwining her fingers as she says the word mesh. "Looking back at my previous relationships, guys, it doesn't even compare, you know?"

"That's how you know when you're really in love. You don't even have to think about it."

She nods.

"That person just becomes this part of you," I continue.

"With Logan, I was always trying to control everything. I wanted things to be perfect. I wanted to look perfect. I wanted us to be this perfect couple with this perfect apartment. But with Martin, I can be myself. I don't need to wear makeup or do my hair and he still looks at me as if I am the most beautiful woman in the world."

"I didn't notice you looking any less fabulous this whole time that he has been living with us," I point out.

"You know I like to look good for me. But I'm no longer doing it for him."

"That's good, Julie. I think that it means that you have a really strong connection."

She nods her head and wraps her arms around herself.

"Everything is just so good right now that it's scaring me."

I smile.

"I mean, you and Jackson are back together -"

"Well, not really."

"You're not?" she asks, surprised.

"We are just taking it easy for now. I still need more time to get over everything."

"Are you telling me that you don't want to be back in his arms again?"

Now, it's my turn to bite my lower lip. "I wouldn't say that exactly."

She laughs and inhales a deep breath.

"What?" I ask. "What's bothering you?"

The lines across her forehead relax and her

face acquires an expression of total serenity. "It just all feels so perfect. I'm worried that if I make one wrong move, it's all going to collapse. Like a house of cards."

I pull her closer to me and bury her head in my shoulders.

"Everything is going to be fine, Julie. We've all been through so much, we deserve a little peace."

———

AFTER WE ARE DONE with dinner, Jackson gives me his hand to help me out of the booth and I don't let it go. Surprised, he gives me a little smile. I pull him closer to me. I miss his touch. I miss his kisses. I miss his smell.

"I miss you," I whisper in his ear.

"I miss you, too."

"Do you mind if we go to your place tonight?" I ask. His eyes light up with anticipation.

"I thought that you would never ask."

When we walk out of the restaurant, our car is already waiting with the valet right at the curb. The door is open and Martin tells Julie and I to get into the back just like we did on the way here.

Julie gets in. I wait for her to move over while Jackson walks around to the driver's seat.

A loud noise that sounds like a car backfiring startles me. Before I get the chance to react, something moving very fast runs into me at full speed, throwing me onto the pavement.

When I open my eyes, my body writhes in pain.

My head is buzzing and I can't get up.

Someone is lying next to me.

I reach for it and when my vision stabilizes, I realize that it's Martin.

His eyes are open and focused on mine.

There's blood streaming down the side of his face from the bullet hole right in the center of his forehead. I close my eyes and everything goes to black.

One-click Tangled up in Love Now!

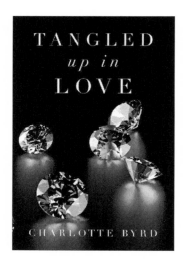

After everything that we have been through, is this finally the end of us?

Our life isn't like other people's.

I crashed into his perfectly ordered world, changing everything. He took my innocence and I taught him that life is better outside the walls of his cloistered mansion.

But then he came along. Parker Huntington is the man who stalked me, attacked me and kidnapped me.

No one has heard from him for a while, and I thought that I was safe. But now he's back with a vengeance.

He will do anything to tear us apart.

What happens if he succeeds?

One-click Tangled up in Love now!

SIGN up for my **newsletter** to find out when I have new books!

You can also join my Facebook group, **Charlotte Byrd's Reader Club**, for exclusive giveaways and sneak peaks of future books.

I appreciate you sharing my books and telling your friends about them. Reviews help readers find my books! Please leave a review on your favorite site.

BLACK EDGE

Want to read a "Decadent, delicious, & dangerously addictive!" romance you will not be able to put down? The entire series is out! 1-Click **Black Edge NOW!**

I don't belong here.

I'm in way over my head. But I have debts to pay.

They call my name. The spotlight is on. The auction starts.

Mr. Black is the highest bidder. He's dark, rich, and powerful. He likes to play games.

The only rule is there are no rules.

But it's just one night. **What's the worst that can happen?**

1-Click BLACK EDGE Now!

Start Reading Black Edge on the next page!

CHAPTER 1- ELLIE

WHEN THE INVITATION ARRIVES...

"Here it is! Here it is!" my roommate Caroline yells at the top of her lungs as she runs into my room.

We were friends all through Yale and we moved to New York together after graduation.

Even though I've known Caroline for what feels like a million years, I am still shocked by the exuberance of her voice. It's quite loud given the smallness of her body.

Caroline is one of those super skinny girls who can eat pretty much anything without gaining a pound.

Unfortunately, I am not that talented. In fact, my body seems to have the opposite gift. I can eat nothing but vegetables for a week straight, eat one slice of pizza, and gain a pound.

"What is it?" I ask, forcing myself to sit up.

It's noon and I'm still in bed.

My mother thinks I'm depressed and wants me to see her shrink.

She might be right, but I can't fathom the strength.

"The invitation!" Caroline says jumping in bed next to me.

I stare at her blankly.

And then suddenly it hits me.

This must be *the* invitation.

"You mean...it's..."

"Yes!" she screams and hugs me with excitement.

"Oh my God!" She gasps for air and pulls away from me almost as quickly.

"Hey, you know I didn't brush my teeth yet," I say turning my face away from hers.

"Well, what are you waiting for? Go brush them," she instructs.

Begrudgingly, I make my way to the bathroom.

We have been waiting for this invitation for some time now.

And by we, I mean Caroline.

I've just been playing along, pretending to care, not really expecting it to show up.

Without being able to contain her excitement, Caroline bursts through the door when my mouth is still full of toothpaste.

She's jumping up and down, holding a box in her hand.

"Wait, what's that?" I mumble and wash my mouth out with water.

"This is it!" Caroline screeches and pulls me into the living room before I have a chance to wipe my mouth with a towel.

"But it's a box," I say staring at her.

"Okay, okay," Caroline takes a couple of deep yoga breaths, exhaling loudly.

She puts the box carefully on our dining room table. There's no address on it.

It looks something like a fancy gift box with a big monogrammed C in the middle.

Is the C for Caroline?

"Is this how it came? There's no address on it?" I ask.

"It was hand-delivered," Caroline whispers.

I hold my breath as she carefully removes the

top part, revealing the satin and silk covered wood box inside.

The top of it is gold plated with whimsical twirls all around the edges, and the mirrored area is engraved with her full name.

Caroline Elizabeth Kennedy Spruce.

Underneath her name is a date, one week in the future. 8 PM.

We stare at it for a few moments until Caroline reaches for the elegant knob to open the box.

Inside, Caroline finds a custom monogram made of foil in gold on silk emblazoned on the inside of the flap cover.

There's also a folio covered in silk. Caroline carefully opens the folio and finds another foil monogram and the invitation.

The inside invitation is one layer, shimmer white, with gold writing.

"Is this for real? How many layers of invitation are there?" I ask.

But the presentation is definitely doing its job. We are both duly impressed.

"There's another knob," I say, pointing to the knob in front of the box.

I'm not sure how we had missed it before.

Caroline carefully pulls on this knob, revealing a drawer that holds the inserts (a card with directions and a response card).

"Oh my God, I can't go to this alone," Caroline mumbles, turning to me.

I stare blankly at her.

Getting invited to this party has been her dream ever since she found out about it from someone in the Cicada 17, a super-secret society at Yale.

"Look, here, it says that I can bring a friend," she yells out even though I'm standing right next to her.

"It probably says a date. A plus one?" I say.

"No, a friend. Girl preferred," Caroline reads off the invitation card.

That part of the invitation is in very small ink, as if someone made the person stick it on, without their express permission.

"I don't want to crash," I say.

Frankly, I don't really want to go.

These kind of upper-class events always make me feel a little bit uncomfortable.

"Hey, aren't you supposed to be at work?" I ask.

"Eh, I took a day off," Caroline says waving

her arm. "I knew that the invitation would come today and I just couldn't deal with work. You know how it is."

I nod. Sort of.

Caroline and I seem like we come from the same world.

We both graduated from private school, we both went to Yale, and our parents belong to the same exclusive country club in Greenwich, Connecticut.

But we're not really that alike.

Caroline's family has had money for many generations going back to the railroads.

My parents were an average middle class family from Connecticut.

They were both teachers and our idea of summering was renting a 1-bedroom bungalow near Clearwater, FL for a week.

But then my parents got divorced when I was 8, and my mother started tutoring kids to make extra money.

The pay was the best in Greenwich, where parents paid more than $100 an hour.

And that's how she met, Mitch Willoughby, my stepfather.

He was a widower with a five-year old

daughter who was not doing well after her mom's untimely death.

Even though Mom didn't usually tutor anyone younger than 12, she agreed to take a meeting with Mitch and his daughter because $200 an hour was too much to turn down.

Three months later, they were in love and six months later, he asked her to marry him on top of the Eiffel Tower.

They got married, when I was 11, in a huge 450-person ceremony in Nantucket.

So even though Caroline and I run in the same circles, we're not really from the same circle.

It has nothing to do with her, she's totally accepting, it's me.

I don't always feel like I belong.

Caroline majored in art-history at Yale, and she now works at an exclusive contemporary art gallery in Soho.

It's chic and tiny, featuring only 3 pieces of art at a time.

Ash, the owner - I'm not sure if that's her first or last name - mainly keeps the space as a showcase. What the gallery really specializes in is going to wealthy people's homes and choosing their art for them.

They're basically interior designers, but only for art.

None of the pieces sell for anything less than $200 grand, but Caroline's take home salary is about $21,000.

Clearly, not enough to pay for our 2 bedroom apartment in Chelsea.

Her parents cover her part of the rent and pay all of her other expenses.

Mine do too, of course.

Well, Mitch does.

I only make about $27,000 at my writer's assistant job and that's obviously not covering my half of our $6,000 per month apartment.

So, what's the difference between me and Caroline?

I guess the only difference is that I feel bad about taking the money.

I have a $150,000 school loan from Yale that I don't want Mitch to pay for.

It's my loan and I'm going to pay for it myself, dammit.

Plus, unlike Caroline, I know that real people don't really live like this.

Real people like my dad, who is being pressured to sell the house for more than a million dollars that he and my mom bought back in the late 80's (the neighborhood has gone up in price and teachers now have to make way for tech entrepreneurs and real estate moguls).

"How can you just not go to work like that? Didn't you use all of your sick days flying to Costa Rica last month?" I ask.

"Eh, who cares? Ash totally understands. Besides, she totally owes me. If it weren't for me, she would've never closed that geek millionaire who had the hots for me and ended up buying close to a million dollars' worth of art for his new mansion."

Caroline does have a way with men.

She's fun and outgoing and perky.

The trick, she once told me, is to figure out exactly what the guy wants to hear.

Because a geek millionaire, as she calls anyone who has made money in tech, does not want to hear the same thing that a football player wants to hear.

And neither of them want to hear what a trust fund playboy wants to hear.

But Caroline isn't a gold digger.

Not at all.

Her family owns half the East Coast.

And when it comes to men, she just likes to have fun.

I look at the time.

It's my day off, but that doesn't mean that I want to spend it in bed in my pajamas, listening to Caroline obsessing over what she's going to wear.

No, today, is my day to actually get some writing done.

I'm going to Starbucks, getting a table in the back, near the bathroom, and am actually going to finish this short story that I've been working on for a month.

Or maybe start a new one.

I go to my room and start getting dressed.

I have to wear something comfortable, but something that's not exactly work clothes.

I hate how all of my clothes have suddenly become work clothes. It's like they've been tainted.

They remind me of work and I can't wear them out anymore on any other occasion. I'm not a big fan of my work, if you can't tell.

Caroline follows me into my room and plops

down on my bed.

I take off my pajamas and pull on a pair of leggings.

Ever since these have become the trend, I find myself struggling to force myself into a pair of jeans.

They're just so comfortable!

"Okay, I've come to a decision," Caroline says. "You *have* to come with me!"

"Oh, I have to come with you?" I ask, incredulously. "Yeah, no, I don't think so."

"Oh c'mon! Please! Pretty please! It will be so much fun!"

"Actually, you can't make any of those promises. You have no idea what it will be," I say, putting on a long sleeve shirt and a sweater with a zipper in the front.

Layers are important during this time of year.

The leaves are changing colors, winds are picking up, and you never know if it's going to be one of those gorgeous warm, crisp New York days they like to feature in all those romantic comedies or a soggy, overcast dreary day that only shows up in one scene at the end when the two main characters fight or break up (but before they get back together again).

"Okay, yes, I see your point," Caroline says, sitting up and crossing her legs. "But here is what we *do* know. We do know that it's going to be amazing. I mean, look at the invitation. It's a freakin' box with engravings and everything!"

Usually, Caroline is much more eloquent and better at expressing herself.

"Okay, yes, the invitation is impressive," I admit.

"And as you know, the invitation is everything. I mean, it really sets the mood for the party. The event! And not just the mood. It establishes a certain expectation. And this box..."

"Yes, the invitation definitely sets up a certain expectation," I agree.

"So?"

"So?" I ask her back.

"Don't you want to find out what that expectation is?"

"No." I shake my head categorically.

"Okay. So what else do we know?" Caroline asks rhetorically as I pack away my Mac into my bag.

"I have to go, Caroline," I say.

"No, listen. The yacht. Of course, the yacht.

How could I bury the lead like that?" She jumps up and down with excitement again.

"We also know that it's going to be this super exclusive event on a *yacht*! And not just some small 100 footer, but a *mega*-yacht."

I stare at her blankly, pretending to not be impressed.

When Caroline first found out about this party, through her ex-boyfriend, we spent days trying to figure out what made this event so special.

But given that neither of us have been on a yacht before, at least not a mega-yacht – we couldn't quite get it.

"You know the yacht is going to be amazing!"

"Yes, of course," I give in. "But that's why I'm sure that you're going to have a wonderful time by yourself. I have to go."

I grab my keys and toss them into the bag.

"Ellie," Caroline says.

The tone of her voice suddenly gets very serious, to match the grave expression on her face.

"Ellie, please. I don't think I can go by myself."

CHAPTER 2 - ELLIE

WHEN YOU HAVE COFFEE WITH A GUY YOU CAN'T HAVE...

And that's pretty much how I was roped into going.

You don't know Caroline, but if you did, the first thing you'd find out is that she is not one to take things seriously.

Nothing fazes her.

Nothing worries her.

Sometimes she is the most enlightened person on earth, other times she's the densest.

Most of the time, I'm jealous of the fact that she simply lives life in the present.

"So, you're going?" my friend Tom asks.

He brought me my pumpkin spice latte, the first one of the season!

I close my eyes and inhale it's sweet aroma

before taking the first sip.

But even before its wonderful taste of cinnamon and nutmeg runs down my throat, Tom is already criticizing my decision.

"I can't believe you're actually going," he says.

"Oh my God, now I know it's officially fall," I change the subject.

"Was there actually such a thing as autumn before the pumpkin spice latte? I mean, I remember that we had falling leaves, changing colors, all that jazz, but without this...it's like Christmas without a Christmas tree."

"Ellie, it's a day after Labor Day," Tom rolls his eyes. "It's not fall yet."

I take another sip. "Oh yes, I do believe it is."

"Stop changing the subject," Tom takes a sip of his plain black coffee.

How he doesn't get bored with that thing, I'll never know.

But that's the thing about Tom.

He's reliable.

Always on time, never late.

It's nice. That's what I have always liked about him.

He's basically the opposite of Caroline in

every way.

And that's what makes seeing him like this, as only a friend, so hard.

"Why are you going there? Can't Caroline go by herself?" Tom asks, looking straight into my eyes.

His hair has this annoying tendency of falling into his face just as he's making a point – as a way of accentuating it.

It's actually quite vexing especially given how irresistible it makes him look.

His eyes twinkle under the low light in the back of the Starbucks.

"I'm going as her plus one," I announce.

I make my voice extra perky on purpose.

So that it portrays excitement, rather than apprehensiveness, which is actually how I'm feeling over the whole thing.

"She's making you go as her plus one," Tom announces as a matter a fact. He knows me too well.

"I just don't get it, Ellie. I mean, why bother? It's a super yacht filled with filthy rich people. I mean, how fun can that party be?"

"Jealous much?" I ask.

"I'm not jealous at all!" He jumps back in his

seat. "If that's what you think..."

He lets his words trail off and suddenly the conversation takes on a more serious mood.

"You don't have to worry, I'm not going to miss your engagement party," I say quietly. It's the weekend after I get back."

He shakes his head and insists that that's not what he's worried about.

"I just don't get it Ellie," he says.

You don't get it?

You don't get why I'm going?

I've had feelings for you for, what, two years now?

But the time was never right.

At first, I was with my boyfriend and the night of our breakup, you decided to kiss me.

You totally caught me off guard.

And after that long painful breakup, I wasn't ready for a relationship.

And you, my best friend, you weren't really a rebound contender.

And then, just as I was about to tell you how I felt, you spend the night with Carrie.

Beautiful, wealthy, witty Carrie. Carrie Warrenhouse, the current editor of BuzzPost, the online magazine where we both work, and the daughter of Edward Warrenhouse, the owner of BuzzPost.

Oh yeah, and on top of all that, you also started seeing her and then asked her to marry you.

And now you two are getting married on Valentine's Day.

And I'm really happy for you.

Really.

Truly.

The only problem is that I'm also in love with you.

And now, I don't know what the hell to do with all of this except get away from New York.

Even if it's just for a few days.

But of course, I can't say any of these things.

Especially the last part.

"This hasn't been the best summer," I say after a few moments. "And I just want to do something fun. Get out of town. Go to a party. Because that's all this is, a party."

"That's not what I heard," Tom says.

"What do you mean?"

"Ever since you told me you were going, I started looking into this event.

And the rumor is that it's not what it is."

I shake my head, roll my eyes.

"What? You don't believe me?" Tom asks incredulously.

I shake my head.

"Okay, what? What did you hear?"

"It's basically like a Playboy Mansion party on steroids. It's totally out of control. Like one big orgy."

"And you would know what a Playboy Mansion party is like," I joke.

"I'm being serious, Ellie. I'm not sure this is a good place for you. I mean, you're not Caroline."

"And what the hell does that mean?" I ask.

Now, I'm actually insulted.

At first, I was just listening because I thought he was being protective.

But now...

"What you don't think I'm fun enough? You don't think I like to have a good time?" I ask.

"That's not what I meant," Tom backtracks. I start to gather my stuff. "What are you doing?"

"No, you know what," I stop packing up my stuff. "I'm not leaving. You're leaving."

"Why?"

"Because I came here to write. I have work to do. I staked out this table and I'm not leaving until I have something written. I thought you wanted to have coffee with me. I thought we were friends. I didn't realize that you came here to chastise me about my decisions."

"That's not what I'm doing," Tom says, without getting out of his chair.

"You have to leave Tom. I want you to leave."

"I just don't understand what happened to us," he says getting up, reluctantly.

I stare at him as if he has lost his mind.

"You have no right to tell me what I can or can't do. You don't even have the right to tell your fiancée. Unless you don't want her to stay your fiancée for long."

"I'm not trying to tell you what to do, Ellie. I'm just worried. This super exclusive party on some mega-yacht, that's not you. That's not us."

"Not us? You've got to be kidding," I shake my head. "You graduated from Princeton, Tom. Your father is an attorney at one of the most prestigious law-firms in Boston. He has argued cases before the Supreme Court. You're going to marry the heir to the Warrenhouse fortune. I'm so sick and tired of your working class hero attitude, I can't even tell you. Now, are you going to leave or should I?"

The disappointment that I saw in Tom's eyes hurt me to my very soul.

But he had hurt me.

His engagement came completely out of left field.

I had asked him to give me some time after my breakup and after waiting for only two months, he started dating Carrie.

And then they moved in together. And then he asked her to marry him.

And throughout all that, he just sort of pretended that we were still friends.

Just like none of this ever happened.

I open my computer and stare at the half written story before me.

Earlier today, before Caroline, before Tom, I had all of these ideas.

I just couldn't wait to get started.

But now...I doubted that I could even spell my name right.

Staring at a non-moving blinker never fuels the writing juices.

I close my computer and look around the place.

All around me, people are laughing and talking.

Leggings and Uggs are back in season – even though the days are still warm and crispy.

It hasn't rained in close to a week and everyone's good mood seems to be energized by the bright rays of the afternoon sun.

Last spring, I was certain that Tom and I would get together over the summer and I would spend the fall falling in love with my best friend.

And now?

Now, he's engaged to someone else.

Not just someone else – my boss!

And we just had a fight over some stupid party that I don't even really want to go to.

He's right, of course.

It's not my style.

My family might have money, but that's not the world in which I'm comfortable.

I'm always standing on the sidelines and it's not going to be any different at this party.

But if I don't go now, after this, that means that I'm listening to him.

And he has no right to tell me what to do.

So, I have to go.

How did everything get so messed up?

CHAPTER 3 - ELLIE

WHEN YOU GO SHOPPING FOR THE PARTY OF A LIFETIME...

"What the hell are you still doing hanging out with that asshole?" Caroline asks dismissively.

We are in Elle's, a small boutique in Soho, where you can shop by appointment only.

I didn't even know these places existed until Caroline introduced me to the concept.

Caroline is not a fan of Tom.

They never got along, not since he called her an East Side snob at our junior year Christmas party at Yale and she called him a middle class poseur.

Neither insult was very creative, but their insults got better over the years as their hatred for each other grew.

You know how in the movies, two characters who hate each other in the beginning always end up falling in love by the end?

Well, for a while, I actually thought that would happen to them.

If not fall in love, at least hook up. But no, they stayed steadfast in their hatred.

"That guy is such a tool. I mean, who the hell is he to tell you what to do anyway? It's not like you're his girlfriend," Caroline says placing a silver beaded bandage dress to her body and extending her right leg in front.

Caroline is definitely a knock out.

She's 5'10", 125 pounds with legs that go up to her chin.

In fact, from far away, she seems to be all blonde hair and legs and nothing else.

"I think he was just concerned, given all the stuff that is out there about this party."

"Okay, first of all, you have to stop calling it a party."

"Why? What is it?"

"It's not a party. It's like calling a wedding a party. Is it a party? Yes. But is it bigger than that."

"I had no idea that you were so sensitive to language. Fine. What do you want me to call it?'

"An experience," she announces, completely seriously.

"Are you kidding me? No way. There's no way I'm going to call it an experience."

We browse in silence for a few moments.

Some of the dresses and tops and shoes are pretty, some aren't.

I'm the first to admit that I do not have the vocabulary or knowledge to appreciate a place like this.

Now, Caroline on the other hand...

"Oh my God, I'm just in love with all these one of a kind pieces you have here," she says to the woman upfront who immediately starts to beam with pride.

"That's what we're going for."

"These statement bags and the detailing on these booties – agh! To die for, right?" Caroline says and they both turn to me.

"Yeah, totally," I agree blindly.

"And these high-end core pieces, I could just wear this every day!" Caroline pulls up a rather structured cream colored short sleeve shirt with a tassel hem and a boxy fit.

I'm not sure what makes that shirt a so-called core piece, but I go with the flow.

I'm out of my element and I know it.

"Okay, so what are we supposed to wear to this *experience* if we don't even know what's going to be going on there."

"I'm not exactly sure but definitely not jeans and t-shirts," Caroline says referring to my staple outfit. "But the invitation also said not to worry. They have all the necessities if we forget something."

As I continue to aimlessly browse, my mind starts to wander.

And goes back to Tom.

I met Tom at the Harvard-Yale game.

He was my roommate's boyfriend's high school best friend and he came up for the weekend to visit him.

We became friends immediately.

One smile from him, even on Skype, made all of my worries disappear.

He just sort of got me, the way no one really did.

After graduation, we applied to work a million different online magazines and news outlets, but BuzzPost was the one place that took both of us.

We didn't exactly plan to end up at the same

place, but it was a nice coincidence.

He even asked if I wanted to be his roommate – but I had already agreed to room with Caroline.

He ended up in this crappy fourth floor walkup in Hell's Kitchen – one of the only buildings that they haven't gentrified yet.

So, the rent was still somewhat affordable. Like I said, Tom likes to think of himself as a working class hero even though his upbringing is far from it.

Whenever he came over to our place, he always made fun of how expensive the place was, but it was always in good fun.

At least, it felt like it at the time.

Now?

I'm not so sure anymore.

"Do you think that Tom is really going to get married?" I ask Caroline while we're changing.

She swings my curtain open in front of the whole store.

I'm topless, but luckily I'm facing away from her and the assistant is buried in her phone.

"What are you doing?" I shriek and pull the curtain closed.

"What are you thinking?" she demands.

I manage to grab a shirt and cover myself before Caroline pulls the curtain open again.

She is standing before me in only a bra and a matching pair of panties – completely confident and unapologetic.

I think she's my spirit animal.

"Who cares about Tom?" Caroline demands.

"I do," I say meekly.

"Well, you shouldn't. He's a dick. You are way too good for him. I don't even understand what you see in him."

"He's my friend," I say as if that explains everything.

Caroline knows how long I've been in love with Tom.

She knows everything.

At times, I wish I hadn't been so open.

But other times, it's nice to have someone to talk to.

Even if she isn't exactly understanding.

"You can't just go around pining for him, Ellie. You can do so much better than him. You were with your ex and he just hung around waiting and waiting. Never telling you how he felt. Never making any grand gestures."

Caroline is big on gestures.

The grander the better.

She watches a lot of movies and she demands them of her dates.

And the funny thing is that you often get exactly what you ask from the world.

"I don't care about that," I say. "We were in the wrong place for each other.

I was with someone and then I wasn't ready to jump into another relationship right away.

And then...he and Carrie got together."

"There's no such thing as not the right time. Life is what you make it, Ellie. You're in control of your life. And I hate the fact that you're acting like you're not the main character in your own movie."

"I don't even know what you're talking about," I say.

"All I'm saying is that you deserve someone who tells you how he feels. Someone who isn't afraid of rejection. Someone who isn't afraid to put it all out there."

"Maybe that's who you want," I say.

"And that's not who you want?" Caroline says taking a step back away from me.

I think about it for a moment.

"Well, no I wouldn't say that. It is who I

want," I finally say. "But I had a boyfriend then. And Tom and I were friends. So I couldn't expect him to—"

"You couldn't expect him to put it all out there? Tell you how he feels and take the risk of getting hurt?" Caroline cuts me off.

I hate to admit it, but that's exactly what I want.

That's exactly what I wanted from him back then.

I didn't want him to just hang around being my friend, making me question my feelings for him.

And if he had done that, if he had told me how he felt about me earlier, before my awful breakup, then I would've jumped in.

I would've broken up with my ex immediately to be with him.

"So, is that what I should do now? Now that things are sort of reversed?" I ask.

"What do you mean?"

"I mean, now that he's the one in the relationship. Should I just put it all out there? Tell him how I feel. Leave it all on the table, so to speak."

Caroline takes a moment to think about this.

I appreciate it because I know how little she thinks of him.

"Because I don't know if I can," I add quietly.

"Maybe that's your answer right there," Caroline finally says. "If you did want him, really want him to be yours, then you wouldn't be able to not to. You'd have to tell him."

I go back into my dressing room and pull the curtain closed.

I look at myself in the mirror.

The pale girl with green eyes and long dark hair is a coward.

She is afraid of life.

Afraid to really live.

Would this ever change?

CHAPTER 4 - ELLIE

WHEN YOU DECIDE TO LIVE YOUR LIFE...

"Are you ready?" Caroline bursts into my room. "Our cab is downstairs."

No, I'm not ready.

Not at all.

But I'm going.

I take one last look in the mirror and grab my suitcase.

As the cab driver loads our bags into the trunk, Caroline takes my hand, giddy with excitement.

Excited is not how I would describe my state of being.

More like reluctant.

And terrified.

When I get into the cab, my stomach drops and I feel like I'm going to throw up.

But then the feeling passes.

"I can't believe this is actually happening," I say.

"I know, right? I'm so happy you're doing this with me, Ellie. I mean, really. I don't know if I could go by myself."

After ten minutes of meandering through the convoluted streets of lower Manhattan, the cab drops us off in front of a nondescript office building.

"Is the party here?" I ask.

Caroline shakes her head with a little smile on her face.

She knows something I don't know.

I can tell by that mischievous look on her face.

"What's going on?" I ask.

But she doesn't give in.

Instead, she just nudges me inside toward the security guard at the front desk.

She hands him a card, he nods, and shows us to the elevator.

"Top floor," he says.

When we reach the top floor, the elevator

doors swing open on the roof and a strong gust of wind knocks into me.

Out of the corner of my eye, I see it.

The helicopter.

The blades are already going.

A man approaches us and takes our bags.

"What are we doing here?" I yell on top of my lungs.

But Caroline doesn't hear me.

I follow her inside the helicopter, ducking my head to make sure that I get in all in one piece.

A few minutes later, we take off.

We fly high above Manhattan, maneuvering past the buildings as if we're birds.

I've never been in a helicopter before and, a part of me, wishes that I'd had some time to process this beforehand.

"I didn't tell you because I thought you would freak," Caroline says into her headset.

She knows me too well.

She pulls out her phone and we pose for a few selfies.

"It's beautiful up here," I say looking out the window.

In the afternoon sun, the Manhattan skyline is breathtaking.

The yellowish red glow bounces off the glass buildings and shimmers in the twilight.

I don't know where we are going, but for the first time in a long time, I don't care.

I stay in the moment and enjoy it for everything it's worth.

Quickly the skyscrapers and the endless parade of bridges disappear and all that remains below us is the glistening of the deep blue sea.

And then suddenly, somewhere in the distance I see it.

The yacht.

At first, it appears as barely a speck on the horizon.

But as we fly closer, it grows in size.

By the time we land, it seems to be the size of its own island.

A TALL, beautiful woman waves to us as we get off the helicopter.

She's holding a plate with glasses of champagne and nods to a man in a tuxedo next to her to take our bags.

"Wow, that was quite an entrance," Caroline says to me.

"Mr. Black knows how to welcome his guests," the woman says. "My name is Lizbeth and I am here to serve you."

Lizbeth shows us around the yacht and to our stateroom.

"There will be cocktails right outside when you're ready," Lizbeth said before leaving us alone.

As soon as she left, we grabbed hands and let out a big yelp.

"Oh my God! Can you believe this place?" Caroline asks.

"No, it's amazing," I say, running over to the balcony. The blueness of the ocean stretched out as far as the eye could see.

"Are you going to change for cocktails?" Caroline asks, sitting down at the vanity. "The helicopter did a number on my hair."

We both crack up laughing.

Neither of us have ever been on a helicopter before – let alone a boat this big.

I decide against a change of clothes – my Nordstrom leggings and polka dot blouse should do just fine for cocktail hour.

But I do slip off my pair of flats and put on a nice pair of pumps, to dress up the outfit a little bit.

While Caroline changes into her short black dress, I brush the tangles out of my hair and reapply my lipstick.

"Ready?" Caroline asks.

Can't wait to read more? **One-Click BLACK EDGE Now!**

ABOUT CHARLOTTE BYRD

Charlotte Byrd is the bestselling author of many contemporary novels. She lives in Southern California with her husband, son, and a crazy toy Australian Shepherd. She loves books, hot weather and crystal blue waters.

Write her here:
charlotte@charlotte-byrd.com
Check out her books here:
www.charlotte-byrd.com
Connect with her here:
www.facebook.com/charlottebyrdbooks
Instagram: @charlottebyrdbooks
Twitter: @ByrdAuthor
Facebook Group: Charlotte Byrd's Reader Club

Newsletter